Returning His Power

Book 3 of the Unconditional Series

By Jacqueline Francis

First paperback edition February 2020

Book design by Romance Novel Covers Now
ISBN (paperback) 978-1-733679954
ISBN (ebook) 978-1-733679947

Books by Jacqueline Francis

Unconditional Series
Book 1 *Returning His Favor*
Book 2 *Returning His Love*
Book 3 *Returning His Power*

Table of Contents

Chapter 1 1

Chapter 2 15

Chapter 3 25

Chapter 4 35

Chapter 5..45

Chapter 6 59

Chapter 7..71

Chapter 8 87

Chapter 9 99

Chapter 10..105

Chapter 11 113

Chapter 12 121

Chapter 13 133

Chapter 14 143

Chapter 15 155

Chapter 16 167

Chapter 17 181

Chapter 18..187

Chapter 19 193

Epilogue 199

About the Author..204

Dedication

To H, for being a wonderful friend, even if there is a big old lake between us!

Chapter 1

The diamond stud nose ring delicately gracing Shannon Grant Romano's face sparkled in the security lights of Grounded. Grounded was Willow Falls, Wisconsin's first and only coffee shop in the small town. It was only 4:30 in the morning, but Shannon had already been up for hours.

Parked in front of the coffee shop, Shannon opened the back of her SUV and pulled out a box of yard signs that said glaringly in red ink, "IMPEACH CARLSON," then dragged them into the front door of the shop. Her petite but strong body pushed the box through the small cafe onto the smooth tiles of the kitchen. Storing them in a back closet, she closed the wooden door and wiped off her hands on her black leggings.

Taking off her hot pink puffy winter jacket and her faux fur earmuffs, she began to wash her hands. Walking over to the industrial ovens, she preheated them all and then got to work on the bakery needed for the day. She pulled her dark brown hair, with some pink strands of hair, into two side buns and slid a baseball cap on her head. As she kneaded the dough to make fresh bread and filled dozens of oversized muffin tins with her famous blueberry batter, she sang along to Billie Eilish. Her playlists consisted mostly of feminist jams and lots and lots of Beyoncé.

Shannon was just pulling the muffins out of the oven, inhaling the familiar scent of fresh streusel and blueberries, when she heard a car door slam out front. It was still early, and Jorge was not due for his shift for another half an hour. Walking out of the kitchen, she rubbed her hands on her white apron, then squinted her blue eyes to see outside in the dark. She groaned as she saw the police cruiser in the early morning light and stormed out to the front door, needing to know what the new police chief wanted with her now.

Unlocking the front door and swinging it open, Shannon was about to scream at the incorrigible chief. Ever since meeting him in the alley when he questioned her Valentine's Day party and her liquor licenses, she had it out for Benjamin Kennedy. Shannon's patience for dealing with male figures of authority was nonexistent, and at least the crotchety old Chief Dick knew Shannon well enough to stay far away.

Ben Kennedy stepped out of the driver's seat and strode around the back of the cruiser. His tall, taut body moved with calculatedness as he walked to the other side of the car. Looking at Shannon, he nodded before opening the back door of the vehicle, stepping through piles of snow. Shannon tried and yet failed to ignore the way that his black uniform pants hugged his muscled— and admittedly amazing—ass. The idea of giving it a firm smack crossed Shannon's mind, then she tucked that idea very far, far away.

Her eyes grew wide as he pulled out about twenty of the signs that she had spent the morning putting up around town, pounding them into the frozen ground. He effortlessly carried them over to her. "I believe these are yours," he drawled in his hint of a southern accent.

"What are you talking about?" Shannon asked defensively, feigning ignorance. She hated to admit that she could feel her cheeks getting redder and redder.

"I have been watching you haul these around town since about three this morning. You can't put up signs on village property about impeaching the Village President," he said matter-of-factly. "Are you trying to cause problems?"

"If you had any idea what kind of monster he is, how much of a rat he is and the extent of his chauvinism —" she began, catching herself before storming into a rant. "Just hand them to me," Shannon said instead, holding out her arms.

"I'll be disposing of these," he said, walking down the sidewalk with them towards the alley. "They have a date with the trash compactor." Shannon glared as he hauled them away effortlessly. She spent hours building those signs and stenciling the letters in. She groaned at the thought of them destroyed.

"There's plenty more where that came from!" She shouted, slamming the front door and locking it loudly. Shannon stormed back into the kitchen and grabbed a muffin, peeling the paper away and biting into the fresh doughy goodness. She normally did not indulge in her own sweets very much, which she considered an occupational hazard, but there was a time and place for a sugar high. The new police chief drove her to this, she told herself.

Leaning against the counter, Shannon stuffed her face with the muffin and sighed at the thought of having to remake the signs. While she had a few left, she was reserving them for on the side of the highway. If she wanted to get real traction in the town, she needed them throughout the village so that people could realize what a pig Carlson really was. Tossing the muffin's paper in the garbage and brushing the crumbs of streusel off of her black shirt, she got to work perking coffee, inhaling the scents of her earthy, dark brews.

Her passion for coffee was what led Shannon to open the shop five years ago. At 23, she borrowed the money from her parents to put a down payment on the abandoned beauty shop, dreaming of being able to serve coffee to the people of Willow Falls. As a lifer in the small Wisconsin town, Shannon knew everyone. Her father's popular construction business was now run by her oldest brother, Phil, after her father retired a few years ago. Her other two brothers, Marco and Jim, also worked for the company. She knew that she could have easily taken a job in the office, but her independent spirit was desperate for something else.

A year into the business, Shannon was able to pay

back her parents for the loan and then some and the business was booming. The closest coffee shop had always been the next town over, a ten minute drive from Willow Falls, and people seemed to love her baked goods.

Shannon did not take much time for herself. Between running the coffee shop and attending various feminist marches and protests in Milwaukee, her head hit the pillow each night in her cute little two story brick house, alone. She liked it that way, she told herself. There was no way that a man would ever tell her what to do again. She was better off alone.

The bell on the front door jingled and Shannon recognized the scuffling of Jorge's Ugg boots on the wooden floor of the shop.

"Morning, boo!" he shouted cheerily to Shannon over the beat of the pop song in the background.

"Hey Jorge," Shannon said with a smile, looking over at her friend and number one employee. Jorge wore tight skinny jeans, probably the same brand that Shannon wore. His fluffy brown boots seemed to top off his outfit. He took off his long parka to show a tight black turtleneck. "How are you today?" she asked him.

"I had about the worst date last night," Jorge explained as he put his parka away and tied an apron around his trim, petite waist.

"The banker?" Shannon asked, intrigued. Jorge nodded as he washed his hands and began getting out ingredients to make sugar cookies. Ignoring the ingredients on the counter, he moved over to the espresso machine to make some for himself, the loud hissing drowning out his deeply sorrowful tale of the hot banker turning out to be the most boring man on Earth.

Shannon clucked sympathetically as she took over making the sugar cookie dough, glancing over at Jorge as he leisurely sipped his espresso and waxed poetic about the lack of eligible bachelors in the area. This was not the first time that Shannon heard about Jorge's complaints and as much as she wanted him to find a nice guy, she couldn't help but smile at the idea of what it would be like for Jorge to finally meet his match. He was the most supportive friend and also the most overdramatic person that she had ever met. It would take a very special person to be able to keep up with Jorge, and she could not wait to see who that was.

The conversation soon turned to Shannon's other dear friends, Melissa and Maddie Danzer. Melissa, the oldest of the two sisters, recently found out she was pregnant with Jakob King's baby. Jakob, a successful mechanic in town, had the unique situation of being ex-Amish. In a turn of events, Shannon had a lifetime's supply of free butter for the coffee shop from his family's farm.

Melissa had been through a lot, and Shannon could not be more happy for her friend. While she did not think that love was for everyone, Melissa was definitely better with Jakob. Another couple that Shannon knew was meant to be is Maddie and Nick, a sexy Scotsman. Shannon had thrown the couple a party for their surprise engagement. Shannon knew just how sad Maddie was when Nick had to go back to Scotland, but she promised to help her with the visa process as much as she could.

When the sugar cookies came out of the oven, she slid them onto cooling racks and walked out to the front door of the shop, turning the closed sign to open and unlocking the door. She turned on the various lamps around the coffee shop, setting the mood. From booths to antique tables, the furniture was an eclectic mismatching of items that Shannon had picked up along the way. Scattered throughout the shop were big cozy chairs in vibrant greens and oranges. Vintage coffee signs hung on the walls and the exposed brick behind the front counter tied it all together.

The cafe was quickly outgrowing the space, which is why she was glad that she snagged up the adjoining office space next door at auction last year. Clear plastic tarps covered the dividing wall between the two spaces, a project that her brothers had helped her with at the beginning of winter. She had plans to expand, making a full-service kitchen so that she could serve a larger breakfast menu and provide much more seating. As a construction worker's daughter, she knew that she could do a lot of it on her own and was excited to get started.

Jorge set to work making coffees for the guests that trickled in steadily. She turned the radio station to coffeehouse music and flipped on the gas fireplace. It was cozy and everything she ever wanted. Clutching a tea towel that she was using to catch stray coffee grounds on the counter, Shannon stepped back and smiled at the bustling coffee shop. She was proud of herself, of her accomplishments, of finally being free.

Shannon strolled back into the kitchen to frost cookies, then packaged them up. She joined Jorge out front, filling the glass case with more pastries and muffins. Busying herself taking orders, she nearly jumped when she realized that time had flown by faster than she thought. Pouring coffee into a travel container and throwing disposable cups and sugar packets into a bag, she grabbed the box of cookies and ran them out to her car.

Running back inside, Shannon shivered at the frigid February air and slipped on her jacket. Saying her goodbyes to Jorge, she slid on the earmuffs and jogged to her car, needing to get to the library as soon as possible.

As the Assistant Director of the Willow Falls Public Library, Maddie asked local business people to run guest storytimes at the library on Saturdays. Shannon was excited to spend time with her friend, even if she did not know much about kids. Sure, she spent time with her nieces and nephews, but that was about the extent of her experience with them. There were women with maternal instincts and then there was Shannon, she told herself.

Pulling into a parking spot, Shannon grabbed her supplies and walked into the library, elated at the blast of nice warm heat the moment she stepped in. Walking into the children's section, she set the coffee and cookies down in the storytime room and proceeded to set up the cups and sugar packets.

Maddie hurriedly walked into the room, looking gorgeous as ever in an emerald green Calvin Klein dress and black nylons, a pair of heeled booties making her look even taller than her natural 5'10". Maddie's blonde hair was swept up in a bun, and she strolled over to Shannon with a clipboard in her hand, pulling a pen out of her bun.

"About time," Maddie said, not bothering to even say hello to Shannon. Shannon bit her lip to hold back a smile. Maddie was all business when she was on the clock.

"So sorry," Shannon said. "It looks like I still have a few minutes. We are fine," she said, reassuring her friend. Checking her watch, Maddie sighed a breath of relief.

"Let's hope we have a good crowd today. Attendance has been lower than normal, probably because of the cold weather. We need to increase our program attendance. I've had posters up and a Facebook event for your storytime, so hopefully that gains some traction," Maddie said, scrawling something on her clipboard.

"Do you have the books for me?" Shannon asked. Nodding, Maddie picked up three books from the storytime chair and handed them to her. Somehow, Maddie was able to come across three picture books about coffee shops. Shannon smiled as she flipped through the pages, admiring the clever and colorful illustrations. Maddie's skills as a librarian never ceased to amaze Shannon.

Children started pouring into the storytime room. Maddie appeared to be simultaneously overjoyed and panicked as she tried to get at least a dozen children to sit properly on the storytime rug.

"Good morning everyone!" Shannon said as she took a seat on the rocker. "My name is Shannon Grant Romano. I own the coffee shop in town, Grounded.

After we read some stories, you all get to have a very special treat that I brought for you." At the news of a treat, the children collectively gasped and *oohed* and *ahhed*. The parents seemed to do the same thing when Shannon told them she had brought coffee for them as well. With a laugh, she began reading.

As much as children were a mystery to her, Shannon found herself really getting into the stories, her love for theatrics revealing themselves in the form of funny voices and lots of body language. The kids laughed at the cute stories and managed to sit through three books. She allowed them to interrupt her several times to answer questions about the coffee shop, and reassured many of them that she did indeed have hot chocolate.

After she finished, she watched the children swarm around the table with the cookies. There were plenty for adults as well so she plated up some for them. A particularly adorable girl who appeared to Shannon to be six or seven years old, strode up to her. Shannon had to laugh at the girl's flamboyant feather boa. Her brown hair in two pigtails, she wore a pair of pink leggings and a black sparkly shirt. The pink boa was the icing on the cake, so to speak, and Shannon could not be more jealous of her outfit.

"I love your style!" Shannon said as she handed the girl a cookie.

"Right back atcha!" the girl smiled, taking the cookie. "I like your nose earring," she said, her toothless grin filling her face.

"Thanks!" Shannon said. "Maybe you can get one

when you're a grownup."

As the child munched enthusiastically on the cookie, she seemed to take a moment to think about it. She shook her head. "Nope, I don't think my Dad would let me," she said. Shannon was about to enter into a discussion about how she did not have to listen to her parents after she turned eighteen but was stopped by a woman moaning into a cookie.

The woman appeared to be in her fifties with naturally graying hair styled into a cute shoulder length cut. She had a trim figure and kind brown eyes. She looked at Shannon suprisingly after she swallowed the bite. "You made these?" She asked, walking up to her.

Shannon nodded. "Yes, I have them in my shop, too."

"These are amazing!" The woman exclaimed. "Aren't they delicious, Amelia?"

The little girl smiled and took another bite, the frosting seeming to get everywhere but in her mouth. "The best," she agreed. Shannon could not deny that Amelia definitely stood out from the rest of the kiddos at storytime. She seemed to be so confident in herself and acted very much like a little grownup.

Maddie came up to them, seemingly relieved now that storytime was over. "What did you two think of storytime?" she asked them.

"It was so good," Amelia said. "This library is much cooler than our old library," she said assuredly. "And these cookies are so yummy. Grandma, do you think we can bake some like these for the cookie competition? They taste so much better than the ones you buy from the store."

Amelia's grandmother blushed as she looked sheepishly at Shannon. "I am not exactly the most talented baker," she explained. "And I guess the first grade cookie competition is a big deal at Amelia's new school. I was just going to pick something up from the Piggly Wiggly," she confessed. "Anything I try to make would be a horrendous disaster. The PTA leader—a Megan Reinhart—she keeps badgering me about it and talking about how competitive it is."

Shannon felt her heartstrings tug as she thought of Amelia having to bring store bought cookies to the infamous first grade cookie competition. She also felt her blood boil at the mention of Megan Reinhart, who was the meanest girl in Shannon's graduating class. For years on end she taunted Shannon about her unique thrifted outfits, cornering her in the bathroom and harassing her with her groupies. Although she hardly knew the girl, Shannon already knew that she would never let Amelia walk into the cookie competition with anything less than the most perfect cookies, if for nothing more than to piss off Megan.

"No," Shannon said assuredly. "She will be bringing in homemade chocolate chip cookies that you two bake yourselves. I will help you," she insisted.

Setting her plate down, the grandmother stepped closer to her. She smelled faintly of honeysuckle. "Oh my heavens," she said. "The people in Wisconsin really are nicer than anywhere else. How I have missed my home!" Stepping forward, she wrapped Shannon up in a hug. "How can I ever repay you?" She asked.

Shannon laughed as she accepted the hug. "It's

no trouble at all," she insisted. "Why don't you come over to the coffee shop around five o'clock tomorrow evening? We close early on Sundays and I already have all the ingredients."

"That would mean the world," the woman said, stepping back to put her hand on Amelia's shoulder, who was now smiling bigger than ever, gazing up at Shannon as if she was a real life princess.

"That's so nice of you," Maddie interjected. "Barb and Amelia have only been in town for a few weeks."

"Miss Maddie," Amelia began, changing the subject. "Do you have any Cary Grant movies at this library?"

Maddie and Shannon laughed at Amelia's question. Usually little girls her age wanted the latest animated feature. Maddie began to explain that she could look it up in the online card catalog, but Shannon interrupted her and asked Amelia if she had ever seen *An Affair to Remember*.

"Of course I have," Amelia said as she put her hand on her hips. "I'm not exactly a newbie to classic films." Loving her attitude, Shannon laughed and decided to test the girl's knowledge.

"What about *The Bachelor and the Bobby-Soxer*? It's Cary Grant with a teenage Shirley Temple." The little girl's eyes grew wide at this.

"I haven't seen that!" She exclaimed, jumping up and down.

"Well you are in luck, missy," Shannon said. "I know for a fact that the library has it because I borrow it all the time. Want me to show you where it is?" Amelia looked up at her grandmother who nodded her approval. Then Shannon and Amelia dashed off to the movie section, enthralled in an intense discussion about Cary Grant's filmography.

When Shannon finally made it back to the coffee shop after a whirlwind morning, she sleepily took out the garbage during the early afternoon lull. As she pushed open the metal door to the alley, she could not help but grin as she saw her signs neatly propped up next to the trash compactor, unharmed.

Chapter 2

Shannon grabbed a protein shake out of the old industrial fridge in the kitchen of the coffee shop. She had bought it for dirt cheap from a defunct restaurant in Fond du Lac. Even though she was constantly getting it repaired or trying to repair it herself, it did the job most of the time. She downed the shake and then began helping Jorge get ready to close up, scrubbing down the coffee machines and getting her clean pans ready for tomorrow morning.

It was a fact, she realized, that the last customer of the day had to be a lingerer. When six o'clock rolled around, there was always one person who needed to finish their crossword puzzle or use the bathroom or just chat to Shannon about town happenings. As much as Shannon loved her customers, she also loved a break.

But there was one person who Shannon always had time for. Margaret Goodrich was one of the sweetest women that Shannon had ever known. She was Shannon's art teacher in elementary school and she always looked up to Margaret for saying what was on her mind. Margaret stood up and walked over to Shannon, a little more slowly since she got her cane. At eighty-five years old, Margaret did everything a little slower nowadays.

"Any news about Mr. Carlson?" Margaret asked Shannon. Margaret was Shannon's biggest supporter in her mission to have Richard Carlson impeached as Village President. Shannon and Margaret had long conversations over tea and cookies about their desire to take him down and get him booted out of office.

"I am going to the Village Board meeting next week to hopefully convince some of them that we need things to change around here, that their leader is a chauvinist and inhumane pig. Will you be there? I can give you a ride," Shannon said, hoping that Margaret would come, if for nothing more than moral support.

"You've got it, kid," Margaret said. "You haven't changed a bit at all," she said with a wink, slowly walking towards the door. Smiling behind her, Shannon locked up and turned the open sign to closed. The street lamps were glowing outside when Jorge was done wiping up the tables. Jorge quickly waved goodbye to Shannon, eager to get ready to go out. Shannon fell into a plush chair by the fireplace, closing her eyes for just a few minutes.

Her impeccably drawn winged eyeliner and purple eyeshadow was smudged after the long day, but none of that mattered anymore. Nestling into the big, overstuffed chair, she easily fell asleep to the sound of the intermittent clanking of the refrigerator, a familiar noise to Shannon.

She awoke with a start at the sound of a banging on the alley door. Pushing her hair out of her face, she stood up and jogged to the door, pulling it open quickly. The blinding brightness of the security light made her pull back her hand to block it from her eyes as she squinted at her brothers. They had backed up their construction truck into the alley and all three of them were starting to unload tools and wood from the back of it.

Marco carried in a saw, bending down to kiss Shannon on the cheek. The brothers all towered over her and their dark, tanned features were a nod to their Italian roots. Phil and Jim carried various beams into the coffeeshop, but not without also bending down to kiss Shannon's cheek. As the little sister of three brothers, she knew that she was spoiled with their overprotective nature. All three of them were married with three children. She got along with their wives, who were all sweethearts. Shannon was happy for them. They were good men, raised by her kind and understanding parents. She really loved her close family, but was glad that she was not tied down with kids like her brothers were.

"Are you sure you can do this on your own, sis?" Phil asked after they had finished unloading all of the materials, slamming the back of the truck shut. "You know we can help out after we finish the school auditorium remodel. We just don't have enough guys right now."

"I can do it myself," Shannon said assuredly.

"Dad taught me everything that he taught you, ya know," she said.

"Yeah, yeah, we know!" Marco teased as he grabbed a leftover muffin from the kitchen counter and walked out into the alley.

"Go get home to your wives and children," Shannon insisted as she shivered in the doorway.

"You get home yourself," Jim said, pretending to order her around although he didn't have a stern bone in his body. The Romano dimples came out when he smiled, and Shannon nodded as she hugged them all goodbye.

"I'm going home in a minute," she assured them. "Just need to turn off some lights." The brothers looked skeptical as they piled into the truck, beeping the horn as they drove off.

Walking back into the coffee shop, Shannon's excitement beat out her exhaustion as she came upon the plastic sheeting. Pulling it back, she stepped into the empty space. The bare white walls were as cold as the snow outside. She could not wait to create the space, to blend it into the current area and make it one big cozy spot to drink coffee, visit with friends, or read a book. Where the world saw drab white walls, Shannon saw potential.

Shannon switched on the ugly overhead fluorescent lights in the new space. Spreading out her construction plans on an old metal desk, she focused in on the doorframe that she needed to finish. Her brothers had taken out enough brick and drywall to make an oversized walkthrough between the two areas. She just needed to fix some of the details and create a half wall to act as a divider.

Shannon grabbed her tape measure from her tool tote and began double-checking her measurements. *Measure twice, cut once*, her father would tell her over and over when she was younger and helping him out at the construction sites. He let her first use a circular saw when she was eleven, but only after promising to never tell her mother. With a nod, young Shannon gathered up all of the energy coursing through her veins and went to town with the saw, getting the biggest thrill as she held the saw, her father's hand gently guiding her cut. When she sliced through a two by four, Shannon had never felt like more of a little badass. It was all over for her after that, and she got her hands on every power tool she could find.

Smiling back at the memory, Shannon propped up her two by fours on the desk, using a pencil to mark her cuts. Plugging in the saw, she began cutting beam after beam.

Before long, she was caught up in the swing of things. She began to mount the two-by-fours to the floor with screws and attached them to the drywall until she was certain they were sturdy. Inspecting her work with the level, Shannon nodded to herself as she tucked the pencil behind her ear. Beginning to sweat, she tossed her hat to the side and began to frame out the half wall, attaching the wood together with a powerful nail gun.

Time escaped her as she worked long into the night. Before she knew it, her half wall was completely framed out and she was ready to attach MDF board. Stepping back to look at her work, Shannon had to blink rapidly. She was starting to have blurry vision, and shook her head in an attempt to clear out her tiredness.

Keep going, she told herself. *You've got this.*
Sensing movement to the left of her, Shannon told herself that her eyes were just playing tricks on her. When the movement would not cease, she turned her head to look out the large front windows that took up nearly the entire front wall of the space.

She jumped back as she saw Chief Kennedy staring at her through the window, a flashlight in his hand. He threw his hands up in confusion and said something to her, but she could not hear him through the window. Pointing to the coffee shop, she moved through the tarp and into the darkened cafe.

Unlocking the door, she came face-to-face, or rather face-to-chest with him, as she swung open the door. He was even taller when he was standing right in front of her, his muscular body looking even broader in the small doorway. Her line of vision landed on his badge and the patch with his last name on his uniform. *Kennedy.*

Ben tucked his flashlight into his utility belt, conveniently next to his gun. He balanced his hands on the belt, then looked down at Shannon. "What in the hell are you doing here?" He asked her. "I thought somebody was breaking in."

"Well, I own this place," Shannon retorted, putting her own hands on her hips.

"You've made that abundantly clear to me," Ben replied, his smile opening wide, reminding Shannon of something familiar, yet she couldn't quite place it. His teeth were white. His skin was perfect. His hair was perfectly coiffed. Was this man for real? He even had the latest style of shaved hair on the sides of his head but longer hair on the top, swept back to make him look very metropolitan. Shannon swore that the mullet had *just* gone out of style about a year ago in Willow Falls, and the men certainly weren't sporting anything this fancy.

"I'm doing some construction work. It's the only time I can do it without closing my doors to customers and I'm not about to do that," Shannon said defensively.

"What kind of construction?" Ben asked curiously. Shannon opened the door wider and held out her arms as a gesture for him to come inside. He slid past her, and she could not deny that his cologne was tantalizingly sexy. While she refused to admit that Ben was attractive, she could at least recognize a good cologne when she smelled it.

Walking over to the sink, she filled a coffee mug with water and downed it. Ben walked carefully through the tarp and into the new space, admiring her set-up of tools. Looking back at her as Shannon walked through the plastic, he gazed at her, his mouth wide. "You did all this?" he asked.

"Yes," Shannon said. "It's not too difficult."

"You're amazing," Ben said as he stared at Shannon. Her hair was a disaster. Sawdust covered her clothing and she probably smelled like she had just run a marathon, but none of that mattered with him. Shannon could not possibly care less what the new badge in town thought about her.

She snorted into her mug and walked over to the saw, unplugging it from the wall. "I just need to hang up the MDF and then I will be done for the night."

"It's past midnight," Ben said seriously, his voice deep. "You should go home and get some rest. You could hurt yourself."

"You're starting to sound like my mother," Shannon said as she hauled the first board over to the wall.

"Let me help you with that," Ben insisted, darting over to help Shannon line up the board precisely.

"Thanks," she said reluctantly, happy to have an extra hand to hold the board as she nailed it on securely. Soon the two had a system going, and between loud punches of the nail gun, Ben struck up a conversation.

"So what's your beef with the Village President?"

Shannon sighed as she bent down to secure the board near the ground. As she worked, she explained everything from the start. "Well, shouldn't you have your own problems with him? When the fire department needed more room, they kicked the police department out and Carlson's great idea was to put you guys in the old funeral home. You do realize that you'd be driving a hearse if his son wasn't the one who sold the village your police truck, right?" Shannon pushed her hair aside as she sat up on her knees, looking up at Ben.

"He's corrupt and unfair, but the police station isn't my only problem, or even touching the surface of his issues. He runs the cannery in town, and they employ about twenty percent of Willow Falls' population. I know from multiple sources that he refuses breaks for women to pump. That violates multiple federal laws. But he's untouchable. Nobody wants to deal with him because he runs this town. So women either deal with it or quit—or if they refuse to listen to him, they get fired. It's disgusting."

Benjamin scowled more and more as Shannon told her story. "He seemed like such a nice guy when I first met him," he said. "My Uncle Dick only had nice things to say about him."

Shannon's eyes grew wide. "Chief Dick is your uncle?" She asked.

Ben nodded. "My great uncle."

Shannon seemed to soften a bit after that. She really liked Chief Dick and even made him coffee when they were both working late into the night.

"Well, anyway," Shannon said, "It's a typical small town boys club mentality. They all work together to scratch each others' backs."

"But what about the funeral home police station?" Ben asked, feeling defensive of his uncle.

"After that happened, Dick told me that Carlson agreed to double his vacation hours and gave him a pretty hefty Christmas bonus with some of the money the village saved on a new police station."

Ben furrowed his brow, upset at the news. "This is terrible," he said. "I can hardly believe it, but it would explain Dick's extended vacations to visit us in Florida."

"Don't blame Dick too much," Shannon said. "It's Carlson's fault. People are scared of him, of pushing back. Someone needs to stop him."

"And you think that person will be you?" Ben asked, reaching out a hand to help Shannon up. She brushed off his hand and used the new wall she built to heft her tired body off the floor. As she walked him to the door, flipping off the lights as she left the new addition, she nodded.

"I *know* it will be me," she said. She thanked Ben for his help, then watched him walk out to his truck. He looked over his shoulder at her, a bit of concern furrowing his brow.

Shannon made sure everything was locked up before leaving the shop and sliding into her SUV. Ben's truck was now parked down the street in front of the station. She imagined him all alone in the creepy police station and felt a little bad for him.

Before she could give it more thought, she drove a quick two minutes to her house. Climbing the steps up to her bedroom, she set her alarm for four in the morning before passing out, barely remembering to strip off her dirty clothes before her body hit the bed.

Chapter 3

Sunday morning went by quickly at the coffee shop. Customers trickled in steadily with a rush after church let out. It was snowing lightly but it hardly stuck to the pavement, so that did not slow anybody down. When it began to dwindle, Shannon peeled off her apron to reveal a tight hot pink skirt and a long sleeved black blouse. A pair of coordinating hot pink pumps with black bows topped off the outfit, bringing it all together.

Shannon woke up refreshed and feeling like she was back to her old self after a few hours of good sleep, and her outfits typically reflected her mood. Yesterday she was feeling pretty drab. Today, she was ready for fun and to spend time with friends. She was also looking forward to baking with Amelia and Barb.

Waving goodbye to Jorge, she strolled down the sidewalk towards one of the local pubs to meet Melissa and Jakob—along with Maddie—for lunch. When she walked into the bustling pub, she quickly saw Jakob. His large stature made him stick out easily in a crowd. She walked up to their booth and slid in next to Maddie.

"Hey guys," she said as she tucked her jacket behind her. The bunch excitedly greeted Shannon and they launched right into an exciting discussion about Maddie's impending wedding and her fiancé's visa process. She teared up talking about Nick back in Scotland. Shannon rubbed her back gently, then looked over at Melissa and Jakob.

"And you two have your hands full with baby prep?" She asked. They took a moment to put their burger orders in, then eagerly got back to their conversation.

Melissa nodded excitedly and Jakob reached out to clutch her hand on the table, squeezing it tightly. "We are painting the nursery tomorrow—well, Jakob is anyway," Melissa smiled. "We finally decided on a shade of yellow."

"Are you entirely positive you want to keep the baby's gender a surprise? Think of the outfits I could be buying for that baby already if I just knew..." Shannon began, but she knew it was hopeless.

"No, we want to be surprised," Jakob said in his deep, deliberate voice. His brown beard framed his handsome face, his features dark and tanned. "I can't wait," he said excitedly, his white teeth showing as he smiled.

Shannon could not help but smile back. She could hardly believe that her two friends found love so quickly, but was so happy for them. She knew that this was real, and not like some of relationships that she dreaded to think about.

"When Nick gets here, we will have to have lots of double dates!" Maddie said excitedly, clapping her hands together.

"And me," Shannon said with a laugh, her toothy smile stretching from ear to ear. She had no qualms about being the third—or fifth—wheel and enjoyed herself just fine.

"Maybe you will find someone," Melissa said encouragingly.

Shannon shook her head as she took a sip of her Pepsi. "Nah, I am good alone," she said. "I prefer it that way." By now, the girls knew that they should not push the subject, so they instead held up their glasses of soda and said cheers before they dug into their food.

As much as Shannon hated saying goodbye to her friends, she had to admit how excited she was to bake cookies with Amelia. It had been a long time since she bonded so well with a child, if ever, and Amelia reminded Shannon so much of herself at that age. As she walked back to the coffee shop, Shannon had to muse that she was never as confident as Amelia at that age, and wondered what the girl's parents were like.

She pictured Amelia's mother as a high-powered lawyer from the big city, never without a tailored business suit. Perhaps her father was a little more creative, maybe an artist or writer.

All thoughts of Amelia and her family left her mind as Shannon busied herself with supply orders for the week and paying some of the bills. Her eyes grew wide as she watched the money dwindle from her bank account as she transferred funds for the electric bill, and told herself that maybe she did not need as many mood lights on all the time.

When she completed all the tasks on her to-do list, she closed the laptop on her small desk in the tiny, cramped office and stepped out into the coffee shop. Jorge was taking an order for some cappuccinos to-go, so Shannon got to work preparing the drinks. At her core, this was where she thrived the most. Shannon loved the art of crafting delicious beverages for people, taking the time to create artwork on the foam or add an extra spray of whipped cream on a child's hot chocolate.

Even though all of the renovations and long hours made her tired, when her heels clicked over the wooden floor and she handed someone a warm beverage on a cold day, she could not help but smile. Shannon was proud of herself for what she accomplished, even with everything that happened. But that was before, she told herself. She was a different person then.

Around ten minutes before they closed, Amelia ran into the coffee shop and up to the counter, Barb not far behind. "Miss Shannon!" Amelia started, bouncing up and down. "Those movies you told me to watch are so good. Grandma let me stay up late last night watching *The Philadelphia Story*. I think it's my new favorite."

"Isn't it amazing?" Shannon asked, so excited that Amelia enjoyed her recommendations. Slipping a piece of paper out of her apron pocket, she handed it to the little girl. "I made a list of some of my other favorites in case you want to check them out. And they are all at the library."

Shannon could have sworn that Amelia was about to begin crying. The girl inhaled deeply, placed the back of her hand on her forehead, and leaned back dramatically. "Darling, this is too much," she said effortlessly. "I shall treasure it forever," she said, shoving the list in her jacket pocket.

It was difficult, but Shannon managed to stifle a laugh at the girl's dramatics. She may have been the cutest kid that Shannon ever met. "Well, come on back!" Shannon said excitedly. "Want to learn how to make hot chocolate?" The sound of the girl screaming in excitement pierced through the coffee shop and Shannon excitedly walked with her over to the machines.

With hot chocolate in tow, they went back to the kitchen. Shannon opened a closet and pulled out two spare aprons, one for Amelia and one for Barb. Barb tied the apron on the little girl, having to circle the string around her waist two times over. Amelia excitedly agreed to wash her hands and she quietly sang the ABCs to herself as she did so.

Shannon slowly went through the very basic instructions for making chocolate chip cookie dough. Amelia was eager about getting into it and helping, whereas Barb sat back, cautiously paying attention and scribbling down notes in a little notebook that she pulled out of her purse.

"I always add more chocolate chips than the recipe calls for," Shannon said. "It's my top secret tip, though. Can you keep a secret, Amelia?" She asked.

Amelia nodded seriously, as if she was now had the entire weight of the world on her shoulders. Barb

smiled at her and then scribbled down more notes.
Amelia and Shannon spent a few minutes making the
dough into balls, then Shannon gestured to Barb to
come over and try it for herself. She gingerly walked
over to the bowl of dough, then grabbed a palmful, and
made it into a ball. "Don't overthink it," Shannon said
gently. "Just have fun with it."

After placing a few more balls on the cookie
sheet, Barb and Amelia had used up the dough. Walking
over to the oven, Shannon said, "When you use the
oven, it's very important that you ask a grown-up for
help." Amelia nodded seriously and watched as
Shannon slid the cookie sheets in. Her eyes grew wide as
she watched the cookies through the door, as if waiting
for them to instantly bake.

She and Barb tidied up the kitchen as Amelia
kept watch on the cookies. "So Maddie said you two are
new in town? Where did you move from?"

"Down south," Barb said. "But I spent a lot of
time here as a kid. I remember summers at Lake
Michigan. There's nothing like it," she said. "We are
glad to be back."

"And we are glad to have you," Shannon said with
a smile as she tossed a towel over her shoulder.

"I like sledding," Amelia said. "It's so fun. Do you
go sledding?"

Shannon laughed. "I haven't been sledding in
years, but it sure is fun."

"You should come sledding with me," Amelia
said. "Everybody should go sledding."

"That sounds like a perfect idea," Shannon said.
She remembered the thrill of sliding down the big hill at

Lake Park, going faster and faster as she made her way down the hill.

"I think they are almost done!" Amelia said a few minutes later. Walking over to the oven, Shannon checked the cookies and eyed the timer.

"Looks like they need about a minute more, then they will be perfect," she said, placing her hands on the girl's shoulders as she peered into the oven.

"I can't wait!" Amelia said. "They look *soooo* good."

"You know," Shannon said. "As the baker, you have one of the most important jobs still left."

"Oh?" Amelia asked, very curious now.

"Taste testing," Shannon said, nodding as her bob shook from side to side.

Amelia giggled and clasped her hands together, waiting for the timer to go off. When Shannon safely removed the cookies from the oven, Amelia eyed them up adoringly. "They are perfect!" She said.

"In just a minute we will move them to cooling racks and then you can try one!" Shannon said, excited for the little girl. She prepared the cooling racks, then gingerly slid the cookies one by one onto them. When she came upon the last few, she used her spatula to place two on a plate. "Okay, here's your chance to tell me what you think of them," Shannon said.

Barb and Amelia bit into the cookies, their eyes going wide like they did with Shannon's sugar cookies. "They are perfect!" Amelia exclaimed.

Barb set her cookie down and walked over to hug Shannon again. "I don't know how to thank you for helping with this, Shannon," she said. "It truly means the world."

"It's my pleasure," Shannon said genuinely to the woman. "We will put them on a platter so it does not look like you got them from anywhere but your kitchen."

"You're a genius," Barb said. "I got another email from that Megan lady badgering me about the competition. She is certainly taking it seriously."

Shannon squinted her eyes at the mention of Megan, then turned towards Barb. "You want to know a secret about Miss Perfect?" she asked Barb. Barb nodded her head, excited for the gossip. "Megan gets her cookies from the bakery two towns over, which is run by my friend from pastry school. She's a big fraud."

Barb gasped and then plastered a devilish smile on her face. "I will keep that tidbit of information to myself, but it will certainly make it easier to face her at this competition."

"Anything I can do to help," Shannon said with a grin, bending down to find a platter in her overflowing cabinets.

While they waited for the cookies to cool, Shannon gave Barb and Amelia a tour of the coffee shop and showed them her new space. When Amelia saw the big white wall, she said, "Ooh, this is just like when Daddy puts a sheet up on the clothesline in the backyard and we watch movies outside!"

Struck silent with the idea, Shannon's mind went racing a mile a minute as she thought about the big white wall. That's it! She could have black and white movies projected onto the wall in the background of the coffee shop, creating an artsy and romantic mood.

"Amelia!" Shannon screamed. "I could kiss you

right now! That is an amazing idea!" She grabbed the girl's hands and twirled her around the big empty space. The girl giggled as she spun around and around in a circle. Barb laughed as she watched Shannon twirl Amelia, grateful that her granddaughter had made a friend.

After giving Barb and Amelia a quick tour of the rest of the space, they went back into the kitchen and slid the cookies on the platter, then covered it with plastic wrap. She handed the platter to Barb after she put her jacket on. Barb thanked her profusely, and so did Amelia.

"You have to promise to stop by and let me know how they turn out at the competition!" Shannon said.

"Promise I will," Amelia said sweetly as she skipped outside and out to their vehicle.

Shannon turned off the lights in the coffee shop then slid past the plastic and into the new addition, which continued to be a very large work in progress. She could hardly contain her excitement about the movie wall and began sketching out her plans for the projector and the white space. Streaming movies all day long would be so charming. She'd have the closed captions on so people could still watch if they liked but they could keep music playing in the background.

The exhilaration Shannon felt at the new idea swept through her veins as she lost herself in her sketching, planning an eclectic mix of colors for paint on the wall but framing out the white space with bold cranberries and reds. She did not consider herself a designer by any means but liked to think that she had an eye for colors, probably inspired by her passion for clothes.

Thinking of clothes, Shannon went into her office to change into a pair of old gray sweatpants and a yellow Marquette University sweatshirt. She filled up a water bottle and took it into the new space, then picked up a can of red paint and shook it up, getting excited about painting the first portion of the wall.

As she ran the roller over the wall, she took pleasure in the calming feeling of painting. She thought of Jakob painting the nursery, and smiled at the thought of a little Melissa or Jakob crawling around. Then she looked down at her own body and felt a little sad at the thought that it would never happen for her. Pushing the roller up and down, she told herself that it was for the best, that children were not part of her plan anyway. She thought about children long into the night, trying to come to terms with the fact that the future she once thought she would have would never actually exist.

Chapter 4

The lake effect brought in about six inches of snow on Monday, so it was extremely quiet at the coffee shop. Shannon sent Jorge home since there was nothing else for him to do but message guys on his dating apps. He gladly strode out of the coffee shop, barely bothering to say goodbye to Shannon.

Shannon spent the evening continuing to work on the painting. She called it a night at around ten o'clock, an early evening for her. By Tuesday night, she was finding herself very confident in her painting color scheme, so happy with the way things were coming together.

She set the radio to quiet jazz as high school students worked on homework and couples sat huddled together, talking about anything and everything.

Shannon stood at the front counter and looked up costs for new refrigerators on her laptop, letting out a breath as she viewed the prices.

The bell on the door jingled and Shannon looked up from her laptop. Standing up straight, she revealed her gold sweater dress. She wore matching gold flats and big hoop earrings. She even changed the diamond in her nose to a little gold stud. Her eyelids had sparkly eyeshadow, giving her an enticing look.

Amelia and Barb walked in, Amelia's face lighting up when she saw Shannon. "Miss Shannon!" she screeched. "We made the most money at the competition for the field trip to the zoo! Everybody loved the cookies."

Barb walked over proudly and handed Shannon the clean tray. "Megan was pis—, I mean, ticked off," Barb said, catching herself in front of Amelia. Shannon could not help but break into a huge smile and she came around the counter to hug Amelia excitedly.

"I knew you could do it!" Shannon said to the little girl. "You're a natural!" Amelia hugged her back and appeared very proud at the compliment.

"We got some movies from the library. Grandma says there's a big snowstorm coming and we might have off of school tomorrow. I have never seen a snowstorm before, but I made sure that we got the movies from your list!" she said excitedly, grabbing for the bag of movies that Barb was carrying.

Shannon crouched down next to Amelia and went through the movies with her, commenting on some of them and making sure to ask Amelia to report back with her thoughts on all of them.

When they put the movies back in the bag and Amelia stood up, Barb had a twinkle in her eyes. "Amelia's father was a real fan of the cookies," she said.

"That's great!" Shannon said. "He can always stop in and pick some up anytime, or this one over here can make him some," she said, bopping her hip towards Amelia. Amelia giggled good-naturedly and nodded.

"But not without help with the oven," Amelia said seriously, making sure to remember what Shannon told her about oven safety.

"That's right!" Shannon said, pleased that the girl was really listening to her.

Amelia and Barb went on their way, but not without picking up some hot chocolate. The people began clearing out for dinner time, and the snow began coming down heavier. The park across from the coffee shop was covered in snow, and you could hardly see the benches or playground.

A Romano Construction truck pulled up in front of the coffee shop, and Shannon walked out to meet her brother, Jim. He brought in their industrial floor sander and hauled his saw back into his truck. He was just bending down to kiss her goodbye on the cheek when Ben walked in.

He appeared shocked to see Shannon with anyone, but lifted up his eyebrows and walked over to the counter. He eyed her business cards. *Shannon Grant Romano, Owner of Grounded.* He recognized her last name from the name on the construction truck outside, quickly making the connection. On the back of her card was a photograph of cappuccino art in a heart shape. He tucked one of the cards in the pocket of his uniform pants.

Shannon went around the back of the counter. "What can I get you today, Officer?" she asked politely. She noticed that his hair was sprinkled with melting snowflakes, his black uniform not looking nearly warm enough on such a cold night.

Shannon punched the information into the register, ignoring him correcting her about his proper title, her many rings flashing in the lighting. "Looks like it's going to be a nasty one out there," Shannon said. "Do you think the Florida guy in you can handle it?" she asked as she poured his coffee.

"I will be just fine," he said. "But what about you? You're going to go home early tonight, right?" Ben asked inquisitively.

Shannon scoffed at this. "I've been through Wisconsin snowstorms for twenty-nine winters now, I think I can handle it," she said cockily.

When she handed him the to-go cup, he nodded at her. "You just be sure you go home early," he repeated, his blue eyes piercing into hers.

She squinted as she made eye contact with him. "I have four wheel drive," Shannon said stoically. "Not that it's any of your business, but I literally live two minutes away. I think I will be fine."

"Work is never worth your safety," Ben said grittily, pointing his finger at her.

"Don't point your finger at me," Shannon snapped back. "I am a grown woman and can make decisions for myself."

"The roads are going to be covered in ice before dark. Why would you risk it?" He asked incredulously, dropping his finger and clutching his coffee cup.

"You wouldn't understand how important this is to me," Shannon said, looking around the coffee shop. "It's all I have," she admitted, regardless of how sad that sounded.

Ben's features softened at that, and he seemed to understand. Maybe her life was not as great as it seemed, but he could not imagine Shannon living a life that she did not enjoy completely. Perhaps nothing was as perfect as it appeared. He pondered this as he sipped his coffee, then grabbed a piece of paper off the counter and scribbled something down. "This is my direct cell. Call if you need me," he said gently, sliding it towards her.

Saying nothing, Shannon peered down at the piece of paper. When Ben walked out the door, she reached down and crumpled it up, tossing it in the recycling bin.

Not a soul came in before it was time to close the doors, and as she locked up, she eyed the floor sander surreptitiously, as if it was a naughty toy that she wasn't supposed to play with.

Sneaking over to the floor sander, she ran her hands over the metal handles, begging to feel the power under her fingers.

Rushing into her office, she slipped off her dress and tugged on a pair of skinny jeans and an old purple sweater along a pair of black sneakers. She swept her hair up into two low pigtails, happy to have it out of her face. She needed complete concentration on the project at hand.

Turning on her stereo, she blared Alanis

Morrissette and turned towards the sander. She moved her paint cans out of the way, happy with her work and excited to see what she could do with the drab old wooden floors.

After plugging in the machine, she grabbed the two handles and pushed it forward. When she turned the switch, one large circular sander began to spin rapidly, bringing up all the old stain on the flooring and allowing her to give it a fresh start.

Remembering that she needed a mask, she dug through one of the bags that her brother brought along and slipped the mask over her nose and mouth, making sure that it was snug.

Starting in a far corner near her now-dry freshly painted walls, she flipped the red switch on the machine and jumped a little at the power of the vibration.

Smiling under the mask, she pushed the machine forward, dust blowing up from the floors. As she continued sanding the floors, Shannon began to notice the progress that she was making. Things were starting to look up and she continued on, ignoring the windy storm outside. It would be pitch black if not for the street lamps, and she kept her focus entirely on her work.

Around midnight, Shannon took a break to eat a sandwich and stood back to look at her work. She had made progress in over half of the space. The years and years of stain on the floor were just like they were when she pulled up the linoleum from the beauty shop and discovered the wooden floors, destroyed by glue and years of neglect.

As she munched on the sandwich, she sat on a

stool and began to get drowsy. The long nights really caught up with her. She walked up to the counter and scooped up some Colombian beans, putting them in the grinder. Then, filling a filter with the grounds, she began to perk a small pot of coffee to keep herself going.

Shannon took the opportunity while waiting for her coffee to look outside. Over a foot of snow had accumulated and the wind was creating enormous drifts in the road. She figured the plows wouldn't be through until morning.

She had just poured a cup of coffee when she heard the slam of a car door outside. Eyes darting to the front door of her shop, she walked over and looked out the window. A big black pickup was parked outside, with beefed up tires and tinted windows. She had not seen it before. A shiver ran through Shannon's spine. She told herself it was just the cold coming through the glass windowpane.

She nearly jumped when someone began pounding on the front door. "Who is it?" She shouted gruffly through the door.

"It's your favorite police chief," she heard a deep voice reply back. Pulling the door open, she immediately recognized Ben even though he was wearing a dark black parka and a black beanie.

Snow blew into the cafe and a drift was teetering to fall inside. "Come in!" Shannon said, moving to the side so Ben could walk in. He stomped his feet on her entry rug, his heavy duty boots clomping on the floor.

"Thanks," he said. "I saw your light on. I wanted to make sure you were okay." As he said this, he turned to Shannon and something sparked within her when she made eye contact with him. He was covered in snow, but she could practically feel the heat coming off of him.

He towered over her, but she did not feel intimidated at all. She hated it when he bothered her with unnecessary worry, but a little part of her liked it.

"What are you working on?" he asked, peeling off his hat. His perfect hair was just a little messy, and Shannon liked to see him this way. What was getting into her? Was she finally losing it after all the late nights or was he truly as sexy as she thought?

"What?" Shannon asked, not hearing a word he said.

"I asked what you are working on tonight?" he repeated, a lazy smile forming after his mouth drawled out the words a little slower this time.

"Oh," Shannon said, disgusted with herself for getting flustered around him. "I've been sanding the floors. I think they look pretty nice."

"How did you learn how to do all this?" Ben asked, quite impressed as he walked in to check out her work.

"My dad showed me everything I know," Shannon said, coming up next to him.

Ben nodded. "I worked for a restoration company when I was going through the police academy. I've done my fair share of floor sanding. Want me to give it a whirl?"

Shannon eyed him, trying not to look too surprised. The pretty boy from Florida knew how to work a sander? *Interesting.* Amused, Shannon pointed towards the sander. "Give it your best shot, big boy," she said saucily.

She stood back and watched Ben strip off his jacket and gloves, tucking the gloves in the pockets of his jacket and then hanging it up on the coat rack. He walked over to the sander in his full police uniform and flipped the switch.

She had to admit that he knew what he was doing. As much as she hated giving up control, he was no rookie when it came to hard work. His muscles tensed through the sleeves of his shirt as he pushed the heavy sander on the floor.

Before she started to look like she was panting and fawning over him, she went back and poured two steaming hot coffees in her famous oversized mugs. After adding a bit of cream to hers, she drew the mug up to her mouth and blew on the steaming hot coffee to cool it down, then took a hesitant sip. Finding it to be just the right temperature between scalding hot and too tepid, she found herself downing the coffee faster than she thought.

She carried Ben's cup over through the plastic tarp and checked out his progress. He was a fast worker, much faster than the meticulous Shannon, but the quality of his work appeared to be the same. He turned to look up at her and smiled, his long hair falling a bit to the sides. She liked seeing him a little messy. Usually his hair was perfectly set with what she assumed was gel or some sort of pomade, but like this he looked a little more rough around the edges.

She held out the cup of coffee and he switched off the machine. As he strode over to her, she said, "I kept it black, is that good?"

"Perfect," he said, reaching out to grab the mug

as he ran his fingers through his hair with the other hand. Taking a big sip, he sighed contentedly. "Your coffee is the best I've ever tasted."

Shannon scowled at him. "Flattery will get you nowhere," she said grumpily.

"It's not flattery if I am just speaking the truth," he said, his eyes clearly amused.

"Well thank you," Shannon said, impressed that such a city slicker liked her coffee.

"Oh!" Shannon said, remembering something before walking back to the cafe area. When she returned a minute later, she held out a plate of her chocolate chip cookies. "Want one?"

Ben was digging in his pants pocket for something, then pulled out a hair tie. He gathered up his hair and tucked it into a short ponytail gathered on the crown of his head. It took Shannon a minute to realize that she had never been so attracted to the idea of a man with a ponytail than at this very second.

He quickly reached out for a cookie and bit into it. Ben's eyes grew wide as he looked up at Shannon. "*You* made these?" he asked incredulously.

"Yeah, it's really not a big deal," she said, clasping the plate of cookies close to her. "They are just regular chocolate chip cookies."

"No," Ben said quietly. "They are so much more than that." Taking a step closer to her, he dropped the cookie onto the plate and grabbed it from her, setting it on the desk.

"What are you doing?" Shannon asked him, but not before he took one step closer to her.

"Shannon," he whispered. "We need to talk."

Chapter 5

"About what?" Shannon asked, not comprehending why everyone thought her chocolate chip cookies were the best thing on Earth lately. Sure, she used a ton of butter and chocolate, but it was not like that was exactly rare.

Ben stepped forward, his big body coming even closer to hers. "Are you married?" He asked her quickly. "The construction guy in here the other day. Is that your husband?"

"What?" Shannon asked once more. "No, that's my brother. Why?"

Letting out a sigh of relief, Ben realized that he must have been holding his breath the entire time she spoke. "Oh," he said. "I just saw the name on the truck and when he kissed you—" he began.

"It was on my cheek," she said. "And Romano is my father's last name. Grant is my mom's maiden name and technically I wasn't born with a dual last name but I figure I am half of her so it's only fair," she rambled.

"You have no idea how relieved I am," Ben said, tipping his chin down to make eye contact with her.

"Oh?" Shannon asked, looking up at him and putting her hands on her hips. "Why is that?"

"Because I like you. I like your spunk, your drive. It's sexy. You're more beautiful than I could ever try to put into words. And I like to think that maybe, just maybe, even though you act like I am the biggest burr in your side, you might like me a little bit, too?" he asked hopefully.

Shannon looked up him, then licked her lips, catching her bottom lip with her teeth. "I don't know what you're talking about," she said a moment later, her mouth turning into an enormous smile.

"Just to be clear," he said, inching back a bit. "Is that a yes?"

"Yes," Shannon said, happy that he thought to clarify.

"Thank fuck," he whispered, his rough hand moving forward to clutch her chin, just barely touching her smooth skin. Leaning down, his lips met hers with a passionate spark. Shannon stood up on her tiptoes to meet him, her arms naturally reaching up around his neck, clutching on tightly.

They stood there kissing for minutes, exploring each other's mouths. Ben clutched her face in his hands, gently caressing her cheeks with the pads of his thumbs. His lips felt smooth on Shannon's, but behind them was a deeper desire, a desire for something fast and rough.

Shannon's own desires mirrored his own, but perhaps not in the way that he thought. Ben led her over to the brick wall, not breaking the kiss. He leaned his body into hers, placing his hands on the wall on either side of her head. His hips slowly pressed towards hers as they deepened the kiss, their tongues furtively dancing together.

When he leaned even more into her, his hips gyrating toward her sex, Shannon grabbed him by his belt and spun out from underneath him. Ben stood back for a second, shocked. "I'm sorry," he said instinctively, holding his hands up. "Did I go too far?"

"Oh you definitely didn't," Shannon said saucily. "But I want to take you to your limit." His eyes grew wide as Shannon pushed him against the wall—strongly but not roughly—pressing her hands into his belt.

He smiled as he looked down at her. "Oh a little spitfire, are ya?" he asked.

She pressed her hands to his chest, then reached up and gently tugged on his ponytail. "Shut the fuck up and let me kiss you," she said, struggling to take charge when he was so tall above her.

With another full smile, Ben reached down and unfastened his holster, setting it onto the nearby desk. Then, reaching down once more, he grabbed Shannon's ass with both hands and pulled her up into his arms, lifting her up off the ground effortlessly. As he dragged her up along his tall body, she felt his erection through his pants, hitting her in her core before he pulled her up further.

She wrapped her legs around his waist and he grabbed tighter to her ass. Shannon had no fear in him dropping her, and grabbed his face to pull their mouths together. Breaking the kiss, Ben said breathlessly, "So you like to take charge?"

Shannon grinned and leaned into him, pressing her hands into his shoulders as she moved to capture his mouth with her own. "You have no fucking idea." At that, Ben's ass squeezes got a little harder. Shannon took charge of the kiss, controlling the frequency and which direction they would go. She relished in the control, liking the idea of dominating over such a big man. From the feel of the erection poking into her core, she had a hunch that Ben was enjoying it as well.

They stayed this way for some time, comfortable with Shannon calling the shots. After a while, she tapped him swiftly on his shoulder and he slowly dragged her body back down his so that she could stand on her own two feet again.

Once she regained her balance, Shannon grabbed his hand and led him back to her office where a small desk and an exercise ball were cramped into a corner with a love seat along the wall. She pulled him into her arms, then pushed him down on the couch. His eyebrows shot up at this, and Shannon quickly kicked off her shoes and then straddled his lap, her legs stretched wide around his enormous, ripped thighs.

She grabbed his face once again, her petite hands grasping his now-stubbly face, and kissed him powerfully. There was no time to think, no time to worry about what he thought. Instead, she ground her sex on his hard erection that was straining prominently against his pants. His pleasurable groans broke free through the kiss but it was not enough for Shannon. She wanted to make him *moan*.

Ben reached for the bottom of her sweater, trying to pull it off, but she slapped his hands away. Instead, she grabbed his hands in hers and guided them up under her sweater, slowly making their way up to her breasts.

They broke the kiss and they both breathed heavily, foreheads touching. Ben made quick, gentle work of exploring her breasts, clutching them softly, then tweaking her nipples between his fingers. Shannon moaned as he continued to massage her nipples, pulling at them gently.

Unable to control herself any longer, Shannon stripped the sweater off, tugging it over her head and tossing it to the floor. Ben bit his lips as he took in her tight body, his hands roaming up and down. She quickly unfastened the black bra then pulled it off.

Ben's face plunged towards her breasts, his mouth swiftly latching onto one of Shannon's nipples. As he suckled on one nipple, his large hand kneaded her other breast. Shannon's back arched at the immense pleasure running through her veins, completely and totally stimulated.

"Take your shirt off," Shannon ordered as she pulled away from Ben's mouth. With a groan at the absence of her delectable breasts, Ben sat back and began unbuttoning his uniform shirt, not getting it off fast enough.

Shannon hated to admit that she nearly drooled

when she saw Ben shirtless. As much as she despised his position of authority, she could not deny how much she loved his body, which proved to be even more sculpted than she thought.

Ben's taut and trim waist appeared small compared to his built upper body. Shannon ran her fingers along his abs up to his broad shoulders. This was a body built over time, with hours of long work put in at the gym. She leaned down and sank her teeth into his shoulder. Shannon could feel Ben's cock twitch against her core, and she smiled at the thought of teasing him.

Shannon glided her tongue against his chest, swirling her tongue around his nipple. Her hands moved all over Ben's body as she sank to her knees in front of the couch.

She reached to unbutton his pants, then gasped as Ben thrust up so that she could pull them down. His tight black briefs hardly contained his cock, which was begging to stand at attention underneath the fabric. Shannon licked her lips as she reached for his erection, wanting to see it, to taste it.

Ben pulled the band of his briefs down, exposing his cock. It stood thick and tall, girthy in all the best ways. His big hand grabbed it, holding it tight as a bit of precum glistened in the bit of dim light from the office.

Shannon stood up and stripped off her pants, pulling off her hot pink panties not long after. Ben stared longingly at her, the heat and need in his eyes. If anyone in the world had bedroom eyes, Shannon deduced, it was Benjamin Kennedy.

"You're beautiful," Ben murmured, as Shannon moved to sit back on his lap, his cock sliding up against her sex. "But you know that," he said, amazed at the confident, sexy woman on his lap.

"Funny," Shannon said as she began grinding her pussy up against his cock, "I was going to say the same thing about you."

"You're ridiculous," he managed to say between his soft groans.

"You're delusional," she retorted, leaning in to kiss him once more.

Ben's cock became slick with the desire from Shannon's sex. "Condom," he said, breaking off the kiss.

"Do you have one?" She asked.

"I don't typically carry them with me at work," Ben replied.

"That's going to have to change," Shannon said. "I don't have one—wait..." she said, standing up and walking to her desk. " I do have one." She rifled through one of her drawers, completely uncaring that she was naked in front of the police chief. She pulled out a small shadowbox, painted red. It said, "In case of emergency, break glass," and two condoms were behind the glass.

"Jorge gave this to me for my birthday," she said, opening up the back of the box and inspecting the condoms. "They aren't expired," she breathed heavily, a sense of relief in her voice. She tossed the condoms over to Ben, who quickly unwrapped one and slid it on, albeit a little clumsily.

Shannon walked over to him, then straddled him once more. Ben reached out and ran his fingers through Shannon's dark curls, then made contact with her clitoris. Shannon moaned as she rode his hand, wanting more. Slowly, Ben slid a thick finger inside of her, and

Shannon nearly came undone. He began to fuck her with his finger while massaging her clit with his thumb.

Was her heart going to beat out of her chest? She balanced her hands on his shoulders as she continued to ride his hand, gasping as he slid one more finger inside of her. The quick, meticulous motions of his thumb brought Shannon to the edge and she neared orgasm with every new movement.

"Come for me," he begged her, pressing his fingers deeper inside of Shannon's pussy. Before long, the orgasm overtook her entire body, tensing up with the orgasm and then slowly, limb by limb, bringing her back down to earth.

She breathed heavily as Ben slowly slid his fingers out of her, placing his hands on her hips. Shannon clutched his face then leaned into him. "Where the fuck did you come from?" she whispered to him, her breathing still unsteady.

Before he had the chance to answer, Shannon reached down and guided his cock to her sex. In one fell swoop, she took all of him to the hilt, overwhelmed with the shocking realization that his cock was much more than she expected. It took her a minute to get acclimated to his size, but she quickly bounced back and began to slide up and down on his cock, not remembering a time when a man's body had ever taken her breath away like this.

"Give it to me," Shannon said, her eyes narrowing as she looked at Ben. Ben's moans and groans were interrupted by his whispers. "You're so fucking beautiful... so perfect," he said to her over and over.

"Show me," she said, grabbing his wrists and

pulling them above his head, then trapping them with hers against the wall. She felt his cock grow even larger inside of her, and bit her lip in devilish satisfaction. He enjoyed not being in control, and that made her more turned on than Shannon could ever imagine.

"Give me that cock," Shannon said to him, finding her voice and her power.

"Yes, ma'am," Ben drawled. As she continued to hold down his wrists, he began to thrust into Shannon, his hard and deep motions making Shannon forget where she was, what her name was.

There was nothing stopping Ben from wanting to bring Shannon the most pleasure she had ever had in her life. As he continued to deliver thrust after thrust, Shannon threw her head back and moaned. His thick cock stretched her out, making her want more and more. She never wanted this to end, this ultimate pleasure upon her.

Their groans of satisfaction filled the small office, Shannon's back arching as she continued to take everything Ben was delivering. "Shannon, fuck," Ben would whisper between thrusts, his wrists straining against her grip, wanting to touch her all over her body, to press his fingers against her nipples, her delicious clit.

"I'm going to come, Shannon," he said to her, minutes later.

"Come for me, *now*," Shannon ordered, feeling the buildup of another orgasm herself, grinding deep and hard on his cock. Moving against her g-spot over and over built Shannon up. Holding his wrists with one hand, she reached down and rubbed her clit furiously, needing to come once more. With a moan, Ben thrust up thrice in succession, spilling his load deep inside of her.

She pulsed forward as the orgasm spilled through her, finding herself moaning his name. Shannon released his hands and they fell to his sides, completely spent.

Shannon rested her head against his shoulder, leaning against him as they both tried to restore their normal breathing.

"That was amazing," Ben said. "You're full of surprises, aren't you?"

"Something like that," Shannon said as she pulled herself up and slid off of Ben onto the love seat. She stood up and slipped her underwear back on as Ben got up and grabbed his pants, walking to the bathroom to take care of the condom.

When he came back a few minutes, later, he had his radio in his hands and was dressed except for his shirt.

"It really came down out there. We must have gotten two or three feet. There's no way I am getting out tonight," he said as he eyed up Shannon, who had the sweater on and just her underwear.

"You're welcome to crash here," Shannon said. "I've spent plenty of nights on this couch. It's pretty cozy."

"And where will you sleep?" Ben asked curiously, his eyebrow perking up.

"Well, considering we just fucked, I was hoping we could share," she said with a smile.

"I am completely fine with that," Ben said, walking over and pulling her towards the couch. He laid down, his feet hanging off the edge, but pulled her into him, spooning her as her ass rubbed up against him. He reached over to grab his uniform top and covered her shoulders with it, wrapping his leg over hers.

Shannon was suddenly exhausted, the work of the evening catching up with her. She felt Ben's soft breathing on the back of her neck and, before she knew it, fell asleep in the comfort of his strong embrace.

It seemed like no time passed at all when Shannon awoke with a start, the scraping of the plows bringing her out of her deep sleep. She found herself tight in the clutches of Ben's arms, his leg still wrapped around hers. She smiled as she heard his quiet, steady breathing and began to slip out of his grasp, hoping not to wake him. She slid on her pants and began to make coffee for him even though it was only five o'clock.

The snow was still coming down, unrelenting large flakes already covering the roads that they had just cleared. She poured two coffees and brought them back into her office. As she leaned down to wake up Ben, she inhaled his deeply sexy, entirely male scent. His cologne mixed with his naturally enticing aroma trumped even her delicious coffee. She was just about to sneak another whiff of him when Ben's eyes shot open.

"I'm up," he said quickly, sitting up and taking note of his surroundings. When he zeroed in on Shannon holding the coffee, the tension seemed to ease off of his shoulders and he relaxed a bit. "Good morning," he said quietly.

"Good morning to you, Officer," Shannon said. "They just plowed the roads, but it looks like they will be closed again soon enough."

Ben grabbed his radio and turned the channel,

listening to the public works department's communication with each other. "This is *Chief* Kennedy checking in. How's it looking out there?"

A moment later, a voice replied, "Chief, it's not looking great. We've been out since two and it just keeps coming down. Schools are already closed today, but so far there aren't many people on the roads, and if they are, they are in trucks. We will call you if anybody is off the road."

"10-4," Ben said, smiling at Shannon as she handed him the cup of coffee.

"Thank you, Shannon. I really enjoyed last night," he said, a glimmer of hope in his eyes.

"It was great," Shannon said curtly, pretending that she wasn't fascinated with his blue eyes, telling herself that it was great sex, nothing else. It couldn't be anything else.

She picked up her phone and texted Jorge, telling him not to come in today. "I'm not opening today," Shannon said. "It doesn't pay with this weather. People are crazy to go outside if they don't have to."

"Good idea," Ben replied between sips of the coffee.

"You're going to go home, right, and take it easy? You need a day off."

"This is coming from the man who seems to work both day shift and night shift without fail," Shannon retorted.

"I knew what I was signing up for when I took the job. I am still getting the lay of the land," he explained.

"For your information," Shannon said smartly as

she sat on the corner of her desk, "I am indeed taking the day off."

Ben looked relieved at her answer. Finishing his cup of coffee, he stood up and buttoned up his shirt. "I suppose I should get out while I can. Thank you for letting me sleep over," he said.

"It's not like I had any alternative," Shannon said, realizing that she sounded like the world's biggest uber bitch.

Ben scowled at that, then went to the front counter to wash his coffee cup out. After toweling it dry, he put his holster on, then added layer by layer, tying his boots tight. When he opened the front door, the drift tipped dangerously. Grabbing a shovel, he worked his way to his vehicle, then came back and cleared a path to Shannon's car.

Shannon watched him as she prepared him a travel mug full of coffee, filling a thermos with more for later. She grabbed a few leftover muffins from the day before and tossed them in a bag. Throwing on her jacket and her boots, she handed the thermos, mug, and bag to Ben when he returned the shovel.

"I could have done that," Shannon said, "but thank you."

"Anytime, Shannon," Ben said. "I mean it, especially if it means I get coffee and treats," he said with a grin.

As Shannon made her way to her car, trying not to slip, she heard the roar of Ben's truck behind her. She smiled at the thought of Ben shoveling out her car, and eased her way into the road, driving slowly as the snow continued to cover her windshield.

What she needed now, she mused, was a hot shower and her cozy bed. The exhaustion seemed to overtake her body as she made her way home. When she got to her driveway, it was miraculously plowed. For that, she had her brothers to thank. They always were looking out for her and it warmed her heart to have such great men in her life.

In the shower, the hot water poured over her. As she soaped up her entire body with raspberry body scrub, Shannon remembered the feeling of Ben last night as he moved inside her, touching her in the most intimate of places.

By the time she got out of the shower, she was sweating. She told herself it was from the steam and the hot water, but as she collapsed into bed with nothing but her towel wrapped around her body, she hated to admit that there was only one man on her mind.

Chapter 6

Shannon slept for longer than she had since crashing after finals in college. It was 5:30 at night when she woke up, confused on the day, the time of day, and what in the hell had happened in the past twenty-four hours.

When last night's events came flashing back into her mind, she covered her face with a pillow and groaned. *She had fucked the new police chief.* "Way to go, Shan," she mumbled to herself.

She stayed like that in bed for some time, paralyzed with embarrassment, before getting out of bed and throwing a pair of cozy pajamas on.

She ate a piece of buttered toast while checking emails and texts on her phone. When she listened to her voicemail, one was from her mother, asking if she was resting and telling her not to work. Her parents had just gotten back from a vacation in Maui and her mother was eager to catch up. Shannon smiled, then sent her mom a quick text to tell her that she had been relaxing all day. Her mother quickly wrote back, insisting that she come over for dinner the next day. After agreeing, Shannon continued to listen to her voicemails.

Sweet Margaret left her two voicemails, the first with a list of points that she wanted Shannon to address in her speech at the Village Board meeting the following night, and another making sure Shannon remembered that Margaret needed a ride.

Shannon made a pot of coffee, then gave Margaret a call back. She read her the outline of what she wanted to say, and the two tweaked a few things, before Margaret said, "You're going to kick some ass, young lady." Shannon smiled at this. She was happy to have Margaret's approval. She needed the support to help take down Carlson and his sexist, illegal behavior.

She spent the evening working on her speech and catching up on chores around her home. Ever since starting the renovations, she had let things like laundry and dishes go. By the time she was done tidying up, Shannon was already exhausted again. She heated up one of the frozen spaghetti dinners that her mother had brought her and mindlessly watched television, dazed by the local news.

Shannon told herself that she needed to get a good night's sleep before the village meeting. She needed to bring her A game, to show the Village Board members that their leadership was corrupt in all ways possible. Carlson was toxic for the future of Willow

Falls, and she would not tolerate it any longer. Shannon looked outside her window and smiled at her "IMPEACH CARLSON" sign that stood next to her mailbox. She slipped on her boots and jacket and walked out to get her mail. Using a gloved hand, she wiped the snow off of the sign and walked back inside proudly, knowing that she had the proof to take him down once and for all.

By ten o' clock, she was sound asleep back in bed, as if she got no rest at all that day. She told herself that she was just catching up on sleep.

When Shannon woke up the next morning, she texted Maddie and Melissa and asked if they were still planning on coming to the meeting. They both replied quickly, telling her that they would not miss it for the world. Shannon had to smile. Her friends were truly the best and most supportive people in the world. She understood that they were both in complicated positions, with Melissa as a relatively new business owner in town, and Maddie as the librarian, and she would never ask them to jeopardize their careers to speak up against Carlson, but she appreciated them showing up nonetheless.

Shannon used an iron to style her bob into tight pincurls, securing them back with diamond clips. She slipped on a pair of black ponte pants and a blazer over her white shirt. She carried a pair of heels in her bag with her as she walked out the door and climbed into her car, her feet toasty in thick boots.

It was still cold outside, but the snow had stopped falling. Piles of snow were pushed to the sides of the road, making Willow Falls look more like Alaska than Wisconsin. As she drove into town, she thought about Ben some more. Sure, he was hot, but he also was incorrigible. Just another man on a power trip, really. She could not deny that, aside from all that, she was attracted to him. There was something about him, something that went beyond his good looks, that made her tick and as much as she hated to admit it she wanted to find out more. But not a relationship, she told herself. Strictly sex. Nothing more.

Jorge was pulling fresh scones out of the oven, looking cozy in a red cable knit sweater and a pair of gray skinny jeans. "I think this is the first time I've been here before you," Jorge said. "I almost called the police." Shannon nearly choked on the espresso shot she was sipping when he said that.

Clearing her throat, she retorted, "That really would not be necessary."

"I don't know, have you seen the new Chief? Think he plays for my team?" Jorge asked seductively, grabbing a pound of King Farms butter from the fridge.

"No idea," Shannon said, grabbing the butter from Jorge and tossing it on the counter. "Go brew the regular and decaf, please," she said curtly.

"Sheesh. Okay," Jorge said, strutting from the kitchen dramatically.

When they opened up, the biggest news from the townspeople was that one of the plow drivers had apparently taken out seven mailboxes yesterday, a new record. The furious homeowners were apparently planning to go to the village meeting. Shannon scoffed at them as she busily served scones and muffins. Leave it to the people of Willow Falls to flip out over mailboxes but sit aside and do nothing when the town's biggest employer was violating the civil rights of so many.

Shannon knew she was being crabby and maybe even slightly unreasonable, but there was nothing that infuriated her more than when people sat back and let horrible things happen right before their eyes. What were they so scared of? It was no secret that these things were happening, so why was everybody so quick to sweep it under the rug?

As the day went by, she eased up on Jorge, and he seemed to forget her bad mood from the morning. When she stepped into her office to process payroll and count cash, the memories of Ben in this very office came flooding back to her. A tingle shot through her spine as she thought about the pleasure that his body brought her, the way he used his hands and his cock to make her come. It had been a while since she felt the body of a man, since she craved to be touched over and over again.

She dove into her paperwork, hoping that she could forget what happened and move on. She had more important things to focus on than sex, and she could not let it distract her from her goals.

After dropping off a deposit at the bank, she drove to Margaret's house, which was not too far from the Village Hall. Shannon went to Margaret's front door and knocked. When Margaret answered, she was wearing a red beret and a puffy black jacket. The woman had style, Shannon admitted. She helped Margaret to her car, taking care with her cane.

As they made their way to the Village Hall Shannon and Margaret commented about how many cars were already filling the parking lot. Shannon dropped Margaret off at the door, then found a parking spot at the edge of the lot. She quickly switched out her boots for a pair of heeled booties, making her at least three inches taller. While she walked in, she noticed the police cruiser pulling into the lot. Instead of making eye contact, she focused on the cue cards in her hand, mentally reciting all of the points she wanted to make.

As she walked into the Village Hall, which perpetually smelled like old paper and cough drops, she took a seat next to Margaret near the front and took off her jacket. People were murmuring around her, mostly talking about the horror of the Great Mailbox Assassination of the Year. The head of the public works department looked less than pleased, and not-so-subtly spit his chew into a soda bottle.

Minutes later, when the Village Board walked in and took their seats at the front of the room, Shannon could not help but scowl at Carlson. He was an older man in his sixties, but his hair was freshly dyed black, slicked back. *Slimy*, Shannon thought to herself. He wore a Willow Falls High School football sweatshirt and a pair of jeans. All part of the public persona look. Well, Shannon mused, she had something for him.

When the meeting began, she listened to dozens of citizens complain about the plowing that was done. Her neighbor a few doors down, a kind but easily infuriated stay-at-home dad, passed out photographs of his mailbox, which he had built and painted himself to look like a replica of his restored Victorian. Shannon could have sworn he almost teared up as he went on and on describing the long nights he spent building the mailbox from scratch.

"This isn't right," Carlson said. "The people have spoken. We will be fixing all of the mailboxes as soon as the snow melts, isn't that right, Douglas?" Carlson said, pointing at the head of public works. Douglas looked annoyed, yet resigned to his fate and simply nodded his head.

Shannon shook her head as she tried to comprehend this insanity. So Carlson was willing to fix mailboxes but was not willing to give nursing women breaks at work? He was fine with fixing mailboxes but could not spend money to give the police department a new building or the library more funding?

When it was Shannon's turn to talk, she stood up and faced the crowd, slowly unbuttoning her blazer. The white shirt she wore was a little more than plain, and in bold black letters, read "Impeach Carlson." The audience gasped as she showed them her shirt, then turned to the board. Out of the corner of her eye, she spotted Maddie and Melissa on the other side of the room. Maddie was smiling and Melissa gave her a thumbs up.

"Members of the Willow Falls Village Board, I am here as a lifelong resident of Willow Falls and as a business owner to address some serious complaints against your President, Richard Carlson. Not only have some of the decisions that he has made as Village President been less than legal, including voting on motions which bring him direct monetary gain, but he has violated multiple federal laws as CEO of his company. Carlson has denied breaks for breastfeeding women to pump, which is illegal in this state and country. He has fired women for taking their breaks, also illegal. The facts are all here," Shannon said, bringing out her notes.

"Get this woman out of here," Carlson snarled at her. "You don't know what you're talking about, young lady."

"With all due respect," Shannon said, approaching the desk, "I do know what I am talking about. On April 10th of last year you voted right here in this room to purchase the new police and fire vehicles from your son's car dealership, a direct conflict of interest. You pushed the only woman ever on the Board, Susana Miller, away by repeatedly silencing her votes. You are consistently involving your canning company in village business to benefit yourself monetarily. How does nobody else see this?"

The crowd's murmurs began to grow louder as Shannon continued to bring out cold hard facts. "In 2016 when you were reelected, you said that you were going to work to make this community better. Fixing mailboxes is not the way to do this," Shannon implored. "Your blatant sexism and illegal behaviors have gone on long enough. I have emails that prove that you propositioned the old village secretary and you threatened her job if she wouldn't meet you at The Billy Goat for drinks. You must step down or I will fight for you to be impeached. You are a crook in all aspects of the word."

By now, the crowd was buzzing with excitement. The majority of the board members appeared shocked as if this was the first time they were realizing Carlson's disgusting behavior. "Get this woman out of here!" Carlson screamed, standing up and wagging his finger at Shannon. His face grew red as the rage pulsed through his blood. "You are a little liar. Your father should be ashamed of you. Get the hell out of my Village Hall," he roared.

"This is a public meeting," Shannon retorted. "I have the emails," she screamed, passing out copies of the emails to the audience.

"Her three minutes are up," the meek clerk said to Carlson reluctantly.

"Silence yourself!" Carlson roared. "Stop this!" He screamed at her. Shannon ignored him and continued to pass out copies of his emails. "Kennedy, remove her this instant!" Carlson said, spitting as he screamed.

For the first time, Shannon noticed Ben standing in the corner of the room near the door. He looked at Carlson, then at her, then back at Carlson.

"I said everything I needed to say anyway," Shannon said. Looking at the audience, she said, "Take this unjust man down! We need new leadership." The entire Village Board sat stunned as Shannon walked to her seat, picking up her jacket and helping Margaret up.

"That's right, leave," Carlson sneered. Shannon began turning around to get in his face, but felt a gentle hand on her arm. "Escort her home, Kennedy. I don't want her lurking around on my—village—property."

She looked up and Ben was holding onto her, not roughly at all, but in a supportive way. He tipped his head towards the door, then whispered down in her ear. "Stay cool and calm," he said. She untensed her body and Ben let go of her arm, then escorted her outside.

The cold air hit Shannon hard as she stepped into the parking lot. Feeling like she could breathe for the first time, she gulped in the fresh air that was so cold it burned her lungs. Ben took the jacket from her arms and wrapped it around her shoulders.

"Are you okay?" he asked her. Shannon said nothing, not yet able to comprehend everything that went down. Maddie and Melissa came out with Margaret and the three huddled around her.

"You were so freaking amazing!" Melissa said.

"The ultimate badass," Maddie chimed in as she shivered in the cold.

"My hero," Margaret said sweetly. "You are one tough woman."

Shannon couldn't help but smile at the women around her. They enveloped each other in a group hug, Ben standing to the side taking it all in.

"I don't suppose you need to escort *me* home, too?" Margaret asked Ben cheekily.

Shannon could have sworn that Ben was blushing, but in the dark it was hard to tell.

"I'd be happy to," Ben said, "But I have orders to take Shannon home."

"We will drive you home, Margaret," Melissa said with a grin, as they sauntered over to her car. Margaret quickly followed suit, catching onto their intentions.

As they sped out of the parking lot, Shannon stood in front of Ben, suddenly feeling like she had nothing to say.

"Let's get you home," Ben said. "No pit stops," he looked at her sternly. Shannon scowled as she climbed into her car, careful not to slip on the ice in her heels.

Ben followed her out of the lot in his cruiser.

Shannon was pissed. Needing to be escorted home, really? This sort of "punishment" by Carlson was not going to work on her.

As she drove into her garage, Ben pulled up behind her, then slammed the door shut.

"I'm home," Shannon said. "Nothing else to see here. Your job is done."

"I need to make sure you get in safe, especially in those shoes." Shannon looked down at her heels and gave Ben an expression that said *really?*

As they walked to her front door, Ben held her screen door open as she unlocked the heavy wooden door. When she stepped inside and looked back at Ben, something tugged at her heart. "Would you like to keep me company while I drink some whiskey?" she asked him.

With a smile, Ben stepped inside and quickly took off his shoes. Closing the front door behind him, he smiled as he took in Shannon's eclectic decor. It reminded him so much of the coffee shop, with mismatched tables and chairs and photographs filling up the walls. It was a cluster and sensory overload, but somehow it was perfect for her and came together so well.

He followed her into the kitchen, where Shannon had a lowball glass and a bottle of Jack Daniels in front of her. She poured a generous amount in the glass. Looking at Ben, she went to her fridge and pulled out a can of soda for him. He took it, snapped the top open, then clinked it with her glass as she raised hers up. Ben watched as she took a hefty sip of the amber liquor, fascinated with this captivating and mysterious woman.

As he sipped on the soda, he watched Shannon's meticulous movements. She bent over in front of him and he felt the heat surge down to his manhood. The sight of her bent over in front of him sent him spiraling more than he thought it would, the memories of their night together coming slamming back into his mind.

He watched her as she undid the clasps on her heels, sliding her feet out of them. She suddenly was transformed back to her petite self. Ben loved the way that she could be such a powerful figure one minute, literally screaming accusations in front of the town and singlehandedly trying to take down the most powerful man in the village, and the next minute looking so innocent as she stood in her kitchen with bare feet and a bottle of Jack.

"So," Shannon said to him. "This is going to be a bit forward, but do you want to fuck me again?"

Ben gulped, then stepped forward. "What did you say?" he asked, his blue eyes wide.

"You. Me. Fucking." Shannon said, setting down the glass and reaching out to finger the pins on his collar.

Chapter 7

"I'm pretty sure only an idiot would refuse to take you up on that offer," Ben said.

Shannon snorted, then leaned into him, lifting her head to make eye contact with him. "You do something to me," she admitted.

"I feel the exact same way about you," he said softly.

Ben reached out to grab her ass and pull her closer. Shannon stood on her tiptoes to reach his mouth. Ben picked her up, then sat her on the corner of the kitchen counter. She could reach his mouth more easily this way, and he leaned down to kiss her furiously with intent.

Ben placed his hands on either side of her thighs on the counter, falling into her kiss. Shannon wrapped her arms around his neck, the taste of whiskey on her lips practically making Ben feel drunk on her. As she hung her arms around his neck, she wrapped her legs around his hips and gripped them tightly. He picked her up, not being able to stand it anymore. "I need to be inside you," he growled into her ear.

"Upstairs," Shannon said, hardly stopping her playful nips on his neck below his collar. He effortlessly carried her up the stairs and found her room. Ben tossed her on the bed, peeling off his uniform as quickly as he could. Shannon stripped off her clothes, a black pleather bra and a pair of lacy thong underwear underneath the shirt and pants.

Shannon rose up on her knees as Ben sank down next to her. He reached down to slip his fingers into the sides of her thong, then pulled it down forcefully. Shannon moaned as he pushed her down, then sank his head down to meet her sex. His tongue parted her sensitive folds, begging to make contact with her clit. Once he found her most sensitive spot, he swirled his tongue around her clitoris, lapping up her juices.

Shannon let out a moan as Ben surprised her by nipping down on her clit, his gentle bites sending her through the roof. She moaned his name into the abyss as he continued to tease her, to thoroughly corrupt her with his mouth. She had never felt anything like this before.

Remembering who she was, she reached down and grabbed his head, tugging on his hair, gently urging his tongue to go deeper.

Ben reacted positively to this, moving his tongue in and out of her sex. The sounds of him licking and sucking on her pussy filled the room and her quiet sighs and moans grew louder as he continued to tease her clit. He ran his teeth along her clit one last time before Shannon came all over his mouth. When she finished thrusting, she released his head from her hands and allowed Ben to come up to her.

"That was fucking amazing," he said to her, a smile on his face. He quickly kissed her and she tasted her sex on his lips, turned on at how much he enjoyed bringing her pleasure. Gone were the days that she slept with anyone who was not completely and totally interested in going down on her.

She sat up, breaking the kiss, and turning the tables on him. She climbed on top of him, feeling his cock standing up straight beneath her. Shannon looked down at his cock, even larger than she remembered it. Glancing up at Ben's eager face, she bit her bottom lip, then crawled off of him.

Grabbing a hair ribbon off her nightstand and rummaging for a condom in her drawer, she came back to the bed, the thick silky black hair ribbon dangling in her fingers.

"What's that for?" Ben asked curiously.

"You'll see," Shannon said cryptically, climbing back on top of him. As she straddled him, she leaned down so that their noses were practically touching.

"Can I blindfold you?" Shannon asked.

"You want to blindfold me?" Ben asked hesitantly. "Isn't it usually the guy who blindfolds the woman?"

"There is no *usually* when it comes to sex, Ben." Shannon said matter-of-factly. "Is that something you'd be interested in?"

Ben thought about it for a minute, his cheeks rosy pink in the moonlight coming from her bedroom window.

"Yes," he said quietly.

"Okay," Shannon said excitedly. "If you don't like it, just take it off okay?" she said sweetly.

"Got it," Ben said. "But I don't think that will be necessary."

Shannon took the ribbon and gingerly tied it around his head, securing it lightly with a bow. "That good?" she asked.

"Perfect," Ben said, his hands roaming up and down her body.

With a smile, Shannon made her way down his body, a trail of kisses left behind on his hard, sculpted abs.

When she reached his cock, she ran her fingernails around his abdomen until she gripped his shaft with both hands, tugging it tightly. He moaned and his hips left the bed as she began to stroke his cock, her small hands moving up and down. She smiled as she saw the wetness form on the head of his cock, then leaned down and licked it up.

Blowing air on the spot she just licked, a shiver ran through Ben. She enjoyed teasing him, making him suffer so sweetly. Before he had a moment to think, she took his cock in her mouth as deep as she could, loving the groans of pleasure coming from him. She began to suck his cock, her mouth bobbing up and down as she worked to take as much of him as possible.

"Baby," Ben said, reaching out to touch Shannon's hair. She used a free hand to grab his, pushing his hand down on the bed and clasping it tightly in hers.

She continued to suck on his hard cock, moving her mouth up and down, her tongue licking the bottom of his shaft as she went along. When she felt his balls tighten, she released his cock from her mouth, pleasurable groans filling the room. Reaching for the condom, she slipped it on his cock as fast as she could.

Turning around to face away from him, she reached down to guide his cock into her sex, a moan of pleasure escaping her lips as he filled her up. She began to ride him, reaching down to clutch his hands on either side of her. She rode him hard, his cock absolutely taking her over. His thick, hard, manhood throbbed inside of her. She bounced up and down, taking him as deep as she could.

The way his cock brushed against her g-spot was maddening. It continued to bring her to the hilt, to that place of no return, teasing her with pleasure. As she continued to ride his cock, she found herself becoming even wetter at the sounds of his moans, his quiet *oh fucks* that filled the room.

Shannon reached down to rub her clitoris as she rode Ben's cock, leaning forward to switch up the angle. She grabbed his leg with one hand and with the other brought herself to orgasm. Her legs quaked as she came, beginning to lose strength as the pleasure rushed through her.

Ben tore the blindfold off and sat up, grabbing Shannon and pushing her to the side. He came up behind her on his knees and his grip tightened on her hips. Shannon's face was buried in a pillow as Ben smacked her ass, then quickly slid his cock back inside her. With a moan, Shannon bit the pillow to stop herself from screaming at the ultimate pleasure. She nearly came undone when he reached underneath her and found her clit with his fingers, teasing and tugging on her sensitive bud.

Ben brought her to the cliff of pleasure over and over again, finally taking her over the edge just as he thrust inside her one last powerful time, collapsing his sweaty body on top of her arched back. They pulled away from each other and regained their breathing and composure on each side of the bed.

Eyes wide, Shannon realized that she had done it again. She gave in again to this irresistible man. There was absolutely no way that she was about to admit to anyone that this was the best sex of her life or that Ben's cock took her to a different planet. No, nobody could ever know this.

Ben's heavy breathing began to regulate as he looked at her. Sensing her discomfort, he leaned over. "Hey, are you okay?" he asked sensitively, his eyes imploring for her to talk.

"That was great," Shannon admitted. "I needed that, thanks."

"Uh, yeah sure," Ben said. "Me too. I better get back to work, I guess."

"Yeah," Shannon said, walking to the bathroom and shutting the door.

Ben quickly put his uniform back on and walked towards the bathroom door, hesitating before knocking. "Hey Shannon, I am going to head out. Are you sure you're okay?" he asked. "I'm worried. Did I do something wrong?"

"No," Shannon said from behind the bathroom door. "Everything is fine. Just a long day. I think I'm going to take a shower. Let yourself out, okay? The door locks behind you."

"Sure," Ben said, not entirely sure of anything right now. After she heard the front door gently close, Shannon turned on the hot water, slipping under the pelting stream. With a sob, Shannon collapsed to the floor of the shower, letting the tears flow freely now. She wasn't okay, not even a little.

It was hard for Shannon to get out of bed the next morning. She swore that she could smell the peppery sweet scent of Ben on her sheets, and that made her want to strip them off of her bed and put on new ones. She told herself that she would do exactly that after work.

She dressed in a light denim jumpsuit with a belt tied around her waist. Shannon rolled up the long sleeves and paired them with some tan Timberland boots. She straightened her hair and put in a pair of gold studs, switching out her nose piercing for a little gold star stud.

Confidently walking into work, Shannon winked at Jorge who had everything under control. She sneaked into the new space and checked out the progress on the floors. She was so happy with the work that was done. She slipped a mask on and began to vacuum up the dust with a shop vac. With the painting done, she just needed to restain the flooring and then she would be ready to have her brothers come in and start the heavy duty contracting work on installing the new kitchen, which she would admit that she needed help with.

After cleaning up the space, Shannon went into her office and found the projector that she ordered online. She carried it into the new addition. Then she brought a ladder out of the back and set it up in the middle of the room. Carrying a drill and some hardware up the ladder with her, she made quick work of installing the projector onto the ceiling so that it would line up perfectly with the white wall.

She climbed down the ladder, then wirelessly connected her laptop to the projector. She began streaming a movie, then climbed up the ladder again to make final adjustments so that it fit perfectly onto her white screen.

Satisfied with the results, Shannon climbed down the ladder once more, putting it back in storage. When she came back, a little face was peeking out from in-between the plastic sheeting. She smiled as she watched Amelia gazing at Clark Gable flirting relentlessly with Claudette Colbert in *It Happened One Night* on her huge new screen. The girl's piercing blue eyes were wide with glee at the sight of it.

"You can come in," Shannon said, smiling at the girl. Amelia broke herself free of her movie trance and smiled at Shannon. She tore past the plastic sheeting and ran into the room.

"Miss Shannon," Amelia said, practically out of breath. "This is my idea. You made my idea come true!"

"I did!" Shannon said. "I couldn't do it without you. What do you think?"

"It's absolutely perfect, darling," Amelia said,

clutching her hands together. "I couldn't have done it better myself."

Shannon stifled a chuckle at the girl. She was never disappointed with Amelia's dramatics and love for life. Where did this girl come from?

"Have you ever seen this movie?" Shannon asked. Amelia shook her head, her attention already back to the movie.

"Wait here," Shannon said, running into the coffee shop. Barb was at the counter, laughing uproariously with Jorge, who was shamelessly flirting with her, complimenting her on her leggings. Barb laughed as she flipped her gray hair behind her shoulder, touched at the young man's compliments.

When she caught sight of Shannon, she immediately tore herself from Jorge. "Shannon, hon, Amelia isn't disturbing you, is she? Oh, how she has been begging me to bring her here so she could see you again!"

"Not at all, Barb," Shannon said, smiling. "In fact, is it okay if she spends some time with me today? I am not doing any demo work, just taking it easy."

"Oh, Shannon," Barb said, grabbing her chest, tears nearly forming in her eyes. "That is so sweet of you, and I know it would mean the world to Amelia. Do you—do you think it would be okay if I run some errands while you two spend time together? If not, just say the word, I totally understand. You're at work and..."

Shannon cut Barb off. "It would be my pleasure to spend time with Amelia. She's a treasure. You take all the time you need," she said with a smile. Shannon picked up a cozy armchair and carried it to Amelia. She set it down in front of the screen and patted the chair. Amelia smiled and hopped in the chair, entranced with the film.

Barb came and said goodbye to Amelia, promising she would be back soon. Amelia hardly said a word to her, as she was way too fascinated with Mr. Gable's incessant wooing.

Shannon turned up the volume of the movie, then went over her plans for the space. She was waiting to finish the floors until all the kitchen renovation was done. She stepped into the space that would be the new kitchen. It was about three times the size of her current kitchen, and she was so excited to think of the possibilities. Expanding to a full breakfast menu would be major for the coffee shop, but she was confident that the recipes she had been working hard on testing would be a hit.

Her mouth watered as she thought about her cinnamon roll pancakes with the sugary icing drizzle that she made to top them off.

"Hey Amelia?" Shannon asked as she carried a tool tote to the kitchen area.

"Hmmm?" Amelia replied, half listening to her.

"Have you eaten lunch yet?"

"Nope," Amelia replied back.

"Do you like cinnamon rolls?"

"Yes, of course, hon," Amelia said.

"What about pancakes?" Shannon asked her.

"Duh," Amelia said cutely.

"Okay, I'll be back in a few minutes. Come on in by Jorge and I if you need anything, okay?" Shannon said to the girl, walking towards the coffee shop.

"Got it, girl," Amelia replied, not peeling her eyes from the screen.

Shannon smiled as she thought of the little cinephile in the other room. It was so sweet how much she loved old movies. Most girls and boys her age were still obsessed with cartoons and animated movies, but here was a first grader already devouring all things Cary Grant and Clark Gable. She was a unique kid, and Shannon was happy to know her.

Shannon walked into the cramped kitchen and washed her hands, then pulled ingredients out of the cupboard. Mixing everything together in a bowl, Shannon walked to the stove and poured oil in a pan, then began to make the pancakes. The heady aroma of cinnamon and cream filled the room. While the pancakes cooked, Shannon kept her eye on the sizzling batter as she whipped together the sugar glaze.

Once the pancakes were done, Shannon made three plates full, drizzling the glaze on top of the stacks. She poured a glass of chocolate milk for Amelia and brought in the plate to her. Amelia's eyes grew wide as Shannon set the plate in her lap and handed her a fork. "This looks so delicious, Shannon!" she said. Shannon smiled as she watched the girl take a bite, then another. "So so so so good!" Amelia squealed. Shannon smiled at the girl and walked back to the coffee shop.

"Lunch is waiting for you in the back, Jorge," She said to Jorge, who was busying himself grinding more coffee beans. Jorge stopped his work and ran back to the kitchen so fast that Shannon had to laugh.

She kept tabs on the counter for a few minutes

while he took his break, refilling customers' drinks and preparing to-go orders. She was so glad that Amelia was enjoying herself. She got the sense that the little girl was so much like her. Maybe she found it hard to relate to kids her age, maybe her interests were too out of the norm for kids to really want to reach out to her. She wanted Amelia to feel free to be herself here, like this was her safe space.

When Jorge came back out from the kitchen about twenty minutes later, he put his hand on Shannon's shoulder. "If I eat those everyday maybe I can finally attract all the chubby chasers on Grindr around here. So freaking good, Shannon. People are going to go nuts for them." Shannon smiled at Jorge's compliment, then went in to the kitchen to grab a plate for herself.

She sat on a stool next to Amelia as they watched the end of the movie while Shannon ate her pancakes. Amelia stretched out in the chair, then jumped up. "That was so good! They were cute together, dontcha think?" she asked Shannon.

Shannon nodded as she ate the pancakes. "A perfect movie couple for sure. Hey, how's school going? I know you had off for the snow days and today is parent-teacher conferences. What's new? Are you making friends?"

Amelia looked up at the ceiling as if she was pondering her response to this. "School is good. I really like my teacher. She's super nice, but not as cool as you. The kids are okay, but a little...*juvenile*, you know? All they care about is playing silly games at recess and I want to talk about movies or read books. It doesn't really bother me, though. My daddy says that I should always be myself no matter what, so that's what I do."

"Your dad sounds like a really smart man," Shannon said. "Being yourself is so important. The only people that matter are the ones who like you for who you really are, like me and Barb and Maddie at the library. We think you are great. I can imagine that being the new kid in school is hard, but you will get through it. Sooner or later, you'll meet just the right people to be your friends."

"You think so?" Amelia asked her.

Shannon nodded. "I know so," she said.

"Shannon, can I ask you something?" Amelia asked. Shannon was shocked at how timid the girl sounded, and she was nervous for what the little girl was going to ask.

"Anything," Shannon said.

"Would you...would you be my best friend?" Amelia asked hesitantly, her big blue eyes staring up at Shannon eagerly.

Shannon's face broke into a huge smile as she heard what the girl said. "I would *love* to be your best friend," Shannon said. "In fact, I was going to ask you the same thing!"

Amelia jumped into Shannon's arms, nearly breaking the plate in her hand. Shannon set down the plate on the stool and wrapped the girl up in her arms, giving her a tight squeeze. The girl was sniffling."Hey now," Shannon said, "No need to get emotional. We are strong women with work to do," she said. Amelia nodded and followed Shannon into the kitchen.

Shannon spent the next half hour attempting to teach Amelia how to use the big dish sprayer. As Amelia stood on the stool in front of the sink, she managed to get more water everywhere else except on the dirty dishes. Shannon laughed more than she had in a very long time with the little girl.

Before long, Barb came back to pick up Amelia. She gave Shannon a big hug and thanked her again for watching Amelia. "Oh no," Shannon said. "Amelia chipped in around here and did manual labor for me," Shannon teased. "Bring her around anytime, I mean it," she told Barb seriously. The woman's kind smile lit up the room and as Barb and Amelia walked out of the cafe hand-in-hand, Shannon had the sudden realization that she forgot to go to her mother's for dinner last night.

Fishing in her apron pocket for her phone, she saw three missed texts from her mom, asking if she was okay. Shannon quickly replied back that she completely forgot and was too wrapped up with "business." Her mother texted her back that Shannon better be over for dinner that night, and it was an order. Shannon tucked the phone back in her pocket and got to work.

When she was locking up that night, she saw the rumble of a vehicle come down the street, and recognized the lights. It was Ben.

His truck came to a slow in front of the coffee shop. "Hey Shannon," Ben said as he rolled his window down.

"Officer," Shannon replied, tipping her imaginary hat at him.

"You know, my correct title is Chief, right?" Ben asked her.

"Okay, Officer," Shannon replied as she walked to her car.

"You doing okay?" Ben asked, putting his truck in park and walking out to her. "I feel weird about how we left things last night."

"I'm fine," Shannon reassured him. "I was just so stressed about the village meeting. It was a long day, you know?"

"I get that," Ben said, reaching out to grab her arm. Before he could touch her, Shannon retracted her arm back. Ben pulled his arm away, stunned at Shannon's movements.

"It's probably not in your best interest for us to be seen together like this," Shannon explained. "I'm the black sheep and am literally trying to get your boss fired. We need to keep it all business."

Ben pondered the thought for a minute. He understood where she was coming from, but that did not stop him from wanting to touch her.

"I get it," Ben said. "I appreciate you thinking of me. I guess I am still not used to the small town politics."

"There are always eyes around, *always*," Shannon said.

Ben nodded. "So how do we act in public? Cordial? Or should you go back to hating me?"

A couple walked out of The Hound Dog, the rival bar of The Billy Goat, and eyed up the two in front of the coffee shop.

"I really am getting sick of this harassment," Shannon said angrily and suddenly at Ben. "You need to knock it off with the 'random' traffic stops when clearly I am doing nothing wrong." Shannon dramatically stormed to her car door, then opened it. The couple stood on the sidewalk, shamelessly gawking at Shannon and Ben.

"And Officer?" Shannon said to Ben, overly angrily.

"Yes, ma'am?" he replied to her formally.

"Fuck the police!" She retorted, but not before he caught a quick wink from her before she climbed into her car and slammed the door.

And with that, Ben got into his truck and grinned from ear to ear, a smile plastered onto his face for the rest of the night.

Chapter 8

In the early hours of Friday morning, Shannon's coffee shop was filled with employees—both current and former—of Carlson's Canning. They were all caffeinated and ready to enact change. Shannon's friends from the company, some of whom quit, some of whom were fired, and some of whom were still employed, gathered around as Shannon explained the plan. They would be coordinating a protest and strike outside of Carlson's, demanding unionization.

Shannon was no expert at unions, but one of the employees, Holly Jones, was working closely with a nearby union representative and the American Civil Liberties Union to get things going.

The crowd of employees thanked Shannon for her generosity and supplying the coffee and space to prepare for the protest. They all worked on getting their signs ready to carry. When the clock struck six, they crowded into cars and headed to the factory. Their shifts were supposed to begin at six but only a few employees' cars were in the lot.

As the crowd began to march on the street in front of the factory on the edge of town, they quickly gained momentum as some of the office workers began filing into work and seeing them.

Not long after seven, a black Rolls Royce pulled into the lot. Carlson stepped out of his car and slammed the door, marching over to them.

"What's the meaning of this?" he screamed. "Get inside and get to work *now*, or you're all fired." Holly handed him paperwork about their formation of a union, not saying a word to him. Carlson cursed and threw the paper on the ground, then stormed into the office building.

Semis filled with supplies began barreling down the street, needing to get past the crowd in order to drop off deliveries for the factory. They honked their horns at the crowd of protesters, but they did not budge.

Shannon continued to march with the group, feeling empowered as they continued to picket. When the red and blue lights began flying down the road towards them, a few of the protesters reluctantly set their signs down, backing away from the group. "I have kids to feed," a few said. "I can't get arrested!" others pleaded.

Before long, the group was down to five of them, hardly enough to stop the trucks. Throwing down her sign, Shannon decided to take matters into her own hands.

Running into the middle of the street, she sat down, then stretched her body out, making it impossible for the trucks to get around her.

Carlson came out, smirking at the employees that reluctantly walked into the factory. Then he eyed Shannon and glared at her. Ben was standing next to his cruiser, hands balancing on his holster.

"Don't just stand there!" Carlson screamed at Ben. "Arrest them now!"

Ben looked uncomfortable as he assessed the situation. Once again, he was stuck between a rock and a hard place. He walked over towards the protestors, reading their signs. Then he walked over to Shannon, whose tiny body was stretched out to take over as much space on the road as possible. She was practically starfished in the middle of the road, and Ben had to smirk at her.

"What are you doing down there?" He asked her.

"I'm using my right to protest the unjust and illegal actions of Carlson Canning."

"Okay, I totally get it, Shannon, but you have to get out of the street."

"Why?" Shannon asked petulantly.

"It's against village ordinance," Ben said. "You can't obstruct traffic on a village street."

"Are you kidding me? If anything should be against 'village ordinance,'" Shannon said, lifting her hands up to make air quotations, "it should be Carlson over there, Mr. Sleazeball himself."

"Listen, I get it, okay," Ben said quietly, talking through gritted teeth. "But can you *please* just get out of the street. Please," he pleaded.

Shannon pretended to consider the idea, giving Ben a glimmer of hope. "Hmm," she said. "Nope. If you want me out of this street you're going to have to drag my ass off of it," she said.

"I'm getting this all on camera!" Holly shouted from the sidelines. Ben looked over and Holly was pointing her cell phone at Ben, wildly jumping up and down as she shouted at him. "What's your badge number?" She screamed unnecessarily loudly at Ben.

Ben sighed, rubbed his eyes with his thumb and forefinger, then walked over to Holly, politely reciting his badge number and answering all of her questions.

This went on for some time, and Shannon had to admit that her ass was getting cold on the pavement. Some of the semi drivers got out to walk to the gas station for broasted chicken, coming back to enjoy their early lunch and watch the action as they leaned against their cabs.

Ben walked over to Shannon. "Last chance," he said to her.

Shannon simply shook her head, resigned to not let Ben interfere with her presentation. The other picketers agreed to move to the sidewalk, not wanting to get arrested. Holly stood on the sidelines with her cell phone out again, capturing Ben and Shannon.

"Shannon Grant Romano, you're under arrest for violating Village Ordinance 39.02 for obstructing traffic, for protesting without a permit, unlawful assembly, failure to disperse, and refusing to obey a peace officer who is enforcing the Vehicle Code."

Ben attempted to pick Shannon up, who made it as difficult for him as possible, turning her entire body into a giant noodle as he tried to get her on her feet. Pulling the handcuffs from the back waist of his belt, he clutched Shannon's hands behind her and slipped the cuffs on her, keeping them more loose than necessary.

He walked her over to the squad, his hand clutching the cuffs as he opened the back door. "Watch your head," he said to her as he helped her gingerly slide into the back. He read her the Miranda rights, then got into the front of the car.

"Nice show you put on there," he said to her, watching Carlson smugly walk back inside the factory.

"Thank you," Shannon said smartly through the Plexiglas window.

"You know I have to take you to the station, right? You're going to be there for a while. Do you have someone to cover the coffee shop?" he asked, turning around to look at her.

Shannon's heart warmed up a bit at his concern for her business. "Jorge is on all day. I didn't know how long this would take," she explained.

"Off we go," Ben said. Looking back in his rearview mirror, he swore then got out. He opened Shannon's door and tugged her seatbelt over her, clicking it in. Then, looking over at the factory, he slid the handcuff keys out of his pocket and nudged her forward, unlocking them.

Getting back in the car and heading to the police station, Shannon muttered "You know I was just getting used to those," as she rubbed her wrists.

When they pulled up in front of the police station, Shannon laughed as Ben took the cruiser behind the building and pulled up underneath an overhang made for a hearse. He stepped out of the car, tugged on the thighs of his pants, then opened her car door.

Shannon stood up and slid out of the vehicle and Ben clicked her cuffs back on. He led her into the station and then came face-to-face with Wanda Redfoot, the station's dispatcher for the past thirty years. Her curly gray hair and pudgy face was familiar to Shannon, as she was a regular at the coffee shop.

"Shannon Romano!" Wanda exclaimed, her manicured hand covering her mouth in shock. "What in the world have you done?"

"Murder," Shannon said seriously.

"Dear Lord in heaven!" Wanda screamed. "What is this world coming to? Oh your poor mother is going to be devastated."

"Calm down, Wanda," Ben said curtly. "She was just protesting."

Wanda grabbed her chest with relief. "Oh is that all? She does that all the time," she said, waddling over to the water cooler to get a glass of cold water.

"I'll book her," Ben said. "Don't you need to go pick up your grandson from kindergarten now anyway?" he asked.

Wanda nodded, then grabbed her oversized purse. "Yes, Tim gets out at noon. If you need anything, Ben, just call me okay?" Wanda asked. "And behave, young lady!" she said to Shannon, wagging her finger at her.

Shannon grinned at the woman, then allowed Ben to guide her down the hallway. When she was "arrested" for her protests before, Dick usually just drove her away from the scene and dropped her back off at the coffee shop. He never actually brought her back here.

Shannon was weirded out by the old, dark funeral home. They came upon a small room, which she quickly realized must be Ben's office. Ben reached into his pocket and uncuffed Shannon, then nodded at the chair in front of his desk.

His face grew red as he looked down at the chair and snatched a well-worn panda stuffed animal from the chair, tossing it behind his desk.

"Awww you're more of a softie than I thought!" Shannon said, winking at Ben. Instead of sitting on the chair that he cleared for her, Shannon walked behind his desk and sat in his big leather desk chair. She swirled around in it, putting her feet up on his desk.

"Damn, this chair is comfortable. If I were you, I'd sit my ass here all day instead of checking on me every five minutes."

"If you stayed out of trouble for longer than five minutes, maybe I could sit down for a change," Ben retorted, sitting on the desk next to her feet.

He folded his arms across his chest, staring at her. "So I formally arrested you, but you can go home today after I get the paperwork filled out. We don't exactly have a jail here for me to keep you."

"Sounds good," Shannon said, used to the drill.

"Listen, Shannon," Ben said. "I can't get you out of my head. I've never been with a woman like you before. I don't want to make you feel uncomfortable with these lines being so blurry. If you feel uncomfortable with this at all, will you please let me know? I'll do whatever I can to make this okay."

She had to smile at how sweet the gesture was. Ben really was a stand-up guy. "As far as I'm concerned, what you and I choose to do while naked has nothing to do with what you do when you're on the clock in your uniform. I don't feel uncomfortable. I know you're just doing your job, but I really appreciate you saying something."

Ben nodded. "You let me know if your feelings ever change on that, okay?" he asked her, his eyes piercing her gaze.

"You've got it, Officer," Shannon said sassily.

Ben checked his watch, then grabbed his badge and set it on the desk. "As far as everyone is concerned, the *Chief* is on his break now, okay?" he asked her.

"Okay," Shannon said with a devilish smile.

Ben leaned down to catch her chin in his big hand. "I oughta take you over my knee for your sass," he said to her, his voice gruff and dark.

"Oh Ben, Ben, Ben," Shannon said. "In my world, you'd be the one going over my knee," she replied,

Ben's eyes grew wide as he took in her words. "I've never been in a situation like this before," Ben admitted. "I'm usually the one who takes charge in the bedroom. I consider myself to be the dominant one."

"But did you enjoy giving up that control with me?" Shannon asked him, her eyes squinting as she pondered Ben's situation.

Ben thought about it for a moment, then quietly said, "I did. I really did like it. I never thought something like that would be for me. It's so complicated," he began, running a hand through his hair. "I feel this need to watch over you, to protect you, to go all alpha male around you, but when it's just you and I and things heat up, I like the things you do to me. I've never been so turned on in my life than when you placed that blindfold on me or held my arms above me."

Shannon nodded, listening to everything Ben was saying. "You can be both, you know," Shannon explained.

"Both?" Ben said.

"Yeah," Shannon said. "An alpha and a submissive. It's a whole thing," she explained. "There are plenty of men who have alpha, super protective tendencies who enjoy giving up control in the bedroom."

"An alpha submissive," Ben repeated, more for himself than anything. As he pondered it, he stood up. Shannon noticed a bulge in front of his pants and bit her lower lip, looking up at him from the chair.

"Does that interest you?" She asked him.

He nodded, then fell to his knees in front of her. "It does," he said. "Very, very much."

Shannon grinned as she leaned forward and caught his mouth with hers, leaning into his kiss and wrapping her hands around his head, running her fingers through his hair.

Ben kissed her with intent and with passion, putting everything he had into the kiss. It was as if he awakened from a long, relaxing sleep and was rejuvenated, ready to try this new discovery. "Tell me what you want," he growled to her when he broke the kiss.

Shannon raised her eyebrows at this. "Well, first I want you to lock your door, then I want you to come over here and get me off with that tongue of yours," she said seductively.

He groaned as she said the words. Standing up, he leaned down to kiss her once more, then walked to the door. "My pleasure," he hissed as his big, muscular body fell back to his knees, ready to do anything in his power to bring Shannon orgasm after orgasm.

Shannon kicked off her sneakers before Ben pulled down her black yoga pants. He was surprised to find a pair of practical black underwear that appeared to actually cover up her ass. When he looked up at her, Shannon shrugged. "Don't hate on the granny panty," she said to him, narrowing her eyes.

He held up his hands. "I didn't say a word," Ben said. "I love everything you wear, granny panty or not." Satisfied with his response, Shannon pushed her hips off of the chair and slid the panties off, kicking them to the side. With a groan, Ben eagerly buried his head between her legs, needing to taste Shannon once again.

As Ben twirled his tongue around her sex, Shannon's whimpers filled the office. "Yes," she moaned, "just like that." She grabbed his head, running her fingers through his hair. His tongue lapped up her wetness, sucking and teasing her clitoris. There was nothing that could stop the orgasm from quickly building up. With one of his signature bites on her clit, Shannon came undone on the chair, grabbing Ben's head as the quake flew through her body.

Ben grabbed Shannon's thighs, spreading her legs wider as he dove even further between them, his mouth eagerly kissing her pussy, worshipping it.

"Yes, Ben," Shannon said softly, yet firmly, as his tongue slid along her wetness. "You do this to me," she said. "You make me so fucking wet."

With a groan, Ben brought one hand up to her, slowly circling her pussy with his finger as his mouth focused on her clit. He sucked on her clit as he slid a finger inside, making Shannon suck in a deep gasp.

Ben began fucking her with his fingers, wanting her to come again and again. He concentrated his tongue on swirling around her clit, lapping up her arousal.

As another orgasm built up inside of her, Shannon threw her head back as she came again, unable to contain the sounds of her pleasure.

She collapsed back into the chair, completely spent. Ben slid his fingers out of her, then sat back on his legs. "You turn me on so much," Ben said. "I could come right now."

Shannon perked up at this. "Stand up," she ordered him. Ben quickly got to his feet and Shannon grabbed his hands, pulling herself off his chair. Now it was her turn to get on her knees in front of him. She unbuttoned his pants and slid the zipper down, licking her lips as she saw his erection protruding against his briefs.

She slid his briefs down, then grabbed his shaft. She licked the underside of his cock, dragging her tongue from his balls to the tip. "Mmm," she said as she moved to take him in her mouth. "Delicious."

"Fuck," Ben said as she moved her mouth up and down. "I'm not going to last long, Shannon. Eating your pussy was the hottest thing, watching you get your pleasure."

She pulled his cock out of her mouth and

squeezed it. "Then come for me," she ordered, sucking on the head of his cock.

She stroked his cock up and down as she continued to suck on the head. When she felt him tense up, Ben grabbed her hair. "I'm going to come," he groaned. When he spilled inside of her mouth, Shannon moaned with pleasure as she lapped up his cream, not getting enough of him.

With a smile, Shannon licked his cock clean, then stood up. Ben appeared to be sated as he leaned against his desk, tucking his cock back into his pants.

"Jesus, woman," he said. "You're going to kill me."

"No, I'm just a minor criminal, remember?" Shannon said as she slid her clothes back on.

Catching his breath, Ben gained his composure, straightening his back and tidying up the papers on his desk while Shannon got dressed. "I'm just going to run to the ladies room while you write up the papers, okay?" Shannon asked.

"Sure," Ben said as she opened the door and walked down the hall. He was grateful for the moment to compose himself and get back to business. Ben had no doubt in his mind that Shannon Grant Romano would be the end of him, one way or another.

Chapter 9

Shannon waited patiently as Ben wrote up the report on her violations. The old funeral home spooked her out, and she much preferred sitting in the chair by his desk instead of exploring the old building. He printed out the paperwork, then handed it to Shannon on a clipboard to read over.

She nodded as she read, fully understanding that she did indeed break the law. She raised her eyebrows at the ticket fees, but figured it was the cost of fighting injustice.

Signing the papers, she slid the clipboard back to Ben across the desk.

"Listen," Shannon said, "I want to talk to you about something. I really enjoy what we are doing here, but you should know that I am not looking for anything serious in terms of a relationship. I mean, I would really prefer monogamy as long as we continue this, but I don't want to lead you on and make you think that I am looking for more than some mutual satisfaction," she explained.

Ben sat silent for a few moments, taking time to process everything she said. Shannon could not get a good read on his facial expressions and was not sure about what he was thinking. "I understand, that works for me too," Ben finally said. "And monogamy is a must," he explained.

"Good," Shannon said, standing up. "I'm glad we agree on that."

Ben stood up too, moving the clipboard over to the other side of his desk. "So, I'm taking a few days off, so I won't be around town as much, but if you need me, do you still have my number?"

"No," Shannon said honestly. "I threw it away," she said matter-of-factly, tucking her hair behind her ears.

"Why would you do that?" Ben asked.

"You were annoying me," she said, as if that was the most reasonable explanation in the world.

"Well will you at least take it now?" he asked.

"No thanks," Shannon said. "I much prefer the spontaneity, don't you?" And with that, Shannon walked out of his office and pushed open the doors of the police station, walking the two blocks down the street to the coffee shop, where she eagerly met a crowd of supporters and gawkers who were desperate for the latest gossip about her protest.

After calming everyone's nerves and reassuring Jorge that she was not going to get thrown in jail anytime in the foreseeable future, Shannon got to work unloading a shipment of baking supplies.

After putting everything away, she went into the alley to cut down boxes and take out some garbage. As she swung a bag of garbage in the trash compactor, her abdomen felt as if it was on fire. "Ugh," she groaned as she clutched her abdomen.

Doing the math in her head, she figured that she must be getting her period and walked back inside, the heavy door slamming behind her. She vowed to take it easy on herself today as much as possible and to cool it with the renovations, just for the day.

Putting a smile on her face, she walked out to the counter and relieved Jorge for a lunch break. Shannon grabbed some ibuprofen from beneath the register and slipped some with a shot of espresso, not wanting to appear as if anything was out of the ordinary.

By the time she closed that night, Shannon was sweating as she washed off the tables. With the amount of snow falling outside and the tricky heater in the building, she should be freezing. Chalking it up to exhaustion and her hormones, Shannon tossed the rag in a bin of laundry and slid her coat on. As she walked to her car through the inches of snow already on the ground, she could not wait to get home and go to bed with a hot water bottle.

The drive home seemed to take forever. When she finally pulled into her garage, Shannon spaced out as she sat in her parked car and closed her eyes. Something was not right.

It was hard to see as she hobbled towards her house, the blizzard of snow nearly blinding her in the dark. The huge pelts of snow hit her face and got into her eyes. She felt around for her back door, unlocking it as fast as she could.

Shannon made it up the stairs to her bedroom, suddenly dizzy. The room began to spin and she could not figure out where she was, confused by her surroundings. Was this her house? Was she at her parents' home? Where was everyone?

Sweat poured off of her face, her shirt saturated with cold sweat as she reached her bed. She sat down, the pain in her abdomen sharpening. With a groan, Shannon reached for her phone. She would call her mother. Her mom would know what to do. By the time she was able to focus on the screen, Shannon pressed the side button three times in a row, calling 911.

When the dispatcher responded, Shannon fell to the floor, clutching her abdomen. She was able to mumble her address before everything went to black.

In her dream, Shannon was running on a treadmill, going faster than she ever had before. In the gym, something crashed behind her. She tried to turn around while still running, but fell to the ground. Then Ben was screaming her name. What in the world was going on? Suddenly, Shannon realized that she was on the floor of her bedroom, and Ben was next to her on the ground, his face concerned as he palpated her body, looking for any source of injury.

"It's you," she said softly as he picked her up in his arms, hearing him say something into his radio. As he carried her down the stairs, Shannon felt no pain, and drifted off back into the darkness.

Seemingly only minutes later, Shannon's entire body ached as a blinding light woke her up. Eyelids sticky, she lifted her eyebrows until they peeled apart and she cautiously looked around her. The sunlight reflected off the sterile white walls of her room. Everything was blurry and she had no idea where she was. What happened last night? When did she paint her bedroom? And what fresh hell was this with no blackout curtains?

"She's up," she heard from her left. Looking over, she saw Barb poking her head in, then whispering to someone outside the room.

"Barb?" Shannon said, her voice scratchy. "Why are you in my house?"

Barb popped back in the room and walked over to her in a sensible light pink cardigan and some jeans. "Oh honey," Barb said. "You're in the hospital. You had to have an emergency appendectomy. Your appendix actually burst but you're okay. They were able to get to you in time, thank goodness." Barb reached out and squeezed Shannon's hand.

Shannon could hardly believe it. She thought she was just having a bad period. "How did I get here?" she groaned quietly, holding onto Barb's hand.

"Ben brought you in," she explained. "The ambulances couldn't get through in the snowstorm. The roads were all closed, but Ben was able to get through in his truck, then brought you here in a snowplow."

Shannon stared at Barb uncertainly. Then realization hit her. "But why are you here? Is Amelia okay?" Panic swept through her veins as she thought about something happening to little Amelia.

Barb smiled. "Amelia is fine. We were here anyway. Amelia was scheduled for a tonsillectomy today and we had to come in last night to prepare. We were here before the storm hit."

Shannon breathed a sigh of relief, then let her head drop back on the pillow. Ben walked in next to Barb. He was wearing a gray and black flannel shirt, the sleeves rolled halfway up his forearm. His face was scruffy and his eyes looked worried as he looked down on Shannon. "Amelia is doing great," he said to her. "Her tonsillectomy went well and she is already excited about the popsicles she gets to eat. And I am so glad you are, fine too. You really scared me."

"How do you know about Amelia?" Shannon asked, royally confused. First Barb was here, and now she was supposed to believe that Ben rescued her, drove her in a snowplow to the hospital and also somehow knew her little best friend? This was too much for her drugged up brain to comprehend.

Ben's Adam's apple bobbed up and down as he looked at her, then at Barb, then back down to Shannon. Finally, said, "I know about Amelia and her tonsillectomy because she is my daughter."

Shannon drew in a breath as she looked from Ben to Barb, who squeezed her hand and nodded, a stoic smile on her face as she looked at Ben and placed a comforting hand on his shoulder. Finally it all made sense. New in town, the same piercing eyes, the cookies, everything.

Overwhelmed at the connection, Shannon felt the room begin to spin, and Ben's concerned face was the last thing she saw before she fainted once again, the room going dark.

Chapter 10

Shannon eventually awoke to see her parents and brothers huddled around her hospital bed. Her mother squealed as she opened her eyes, the afternoon sun much less torturous than it was that morning. They all stood around her bed and talked about how grateful they were that she was okay. Her father's tired, but relieved face came into view.

"Hey Pops," she said to him. He leaned down to kiss her on the cheek.

"My baby girl," he said sweetly. "You're a tough kid, you know. But don't ever let something like this happen again. Your old man can't take it."

"I promise, Dad," Shannon said.

"We met the nice young man who saved your life in the hallway. What a gentleman he is," her mother said proudly, her light brown hair tied up in a bun.

"I'm very grateful for him," Shannon said.

"I wonder if he knows you are single," her mother pondered, practically winking at her daughter.

"Mom!" All three boys groaned at once. Shannon had to laugh at her brothers.

After they finished up their visit, a nurse came in to check on Shannon and give her some more medication. She wasn't hungry at all, but gladly drank plenty of water.

As the nurse straightened up her bedding, she could hear Ben's laugh from the next room.

"Excuse me," Shannon said. "I think my best friend might be in the room next to mine. Amelia? Do you think you could help me go visit her?" She asked sweetly.

The nurse looked at her, and *tsked*. "You really need to take it easy. Your body has been through a lot, and you're on some heavy meds."

"Please," Shannon pleaded with her. "She's just a little girl."

The nurse could not resist that argument, and she gingerly helped Shannon into a wheelchair. Shannon found herself running her fingers through her hair as they made their way out the room, then caught herself and stopped.

"Knock knock," the nurse announced as she pushed Shannon into Amelia's room. Cartoons played on the television and Shannon saw Amelia first, sitting in bed in pink pajamas and eating a fudgesicle.

Her eyes lit up as she saw Shannon. "Daddy!" She screeched, her voice hoarse. "This is my best friend! What are you doing here, Shannon? Why are you in a wheelchair?"

Shannon smiled as the nurse wheeled her next to Amelia's bed. "I'm here to see you," she said cheerily to the little girl. "And I'm in this chair because I had a little procedure but I am feeling much better now. I will be back to normal soon. How are you?"

"I'm fine," Amelia said. "I get to watch TV and eat popsicles all week," she said proudly. "And my Daddy even took off of work." She reached over and tugged on Ben's shirtsleeve, pulling him closer to her bed.

"Daddy, this is Shannon. Shannon, this is my Daddy," Amelia said proudly.

Shannon squeezed her lips together, then said gently to Amelia, "Your dad and I have already met."

Amelia's eyes grew wide, as did Ben's. "You did?" the little girl asked curiously, her popsicle dripping all over her hand.

"Yes," Shannon said. "He saved my life by making sure I got to the doctor in time."

"Oh my goodness," Amelia said dramatically. "This is spectacular!" she croaked out.

Ben lightened up when he realized that Shannon was not going to give his daughter their torrid backstory, and allowed himself to laugh at his daughter's dramatics.

Before anyone could say anything else, Barb walked back into the room. She carried two cups of coffee and handed one to Ben.

"Ben, your daughter needs some sleep now. Maybe you could take Shannon back to her room?" She asked, practically kicking him out of the room.

Used to his mother's antics, Ben did not bother to

argue, but instead thanked her for the coffee, quickly sipped it, then kissed Amelia on the head as he tucked her into the bed. Barb sat on a chair next to the hospital bed, looking smug as she sipped her coffee.

Ben carefully wheeled Shannon back into her room. A nurse followed them in and helped Shannon go to the bathroom, then left Shannon in the wheelchair as she insisted she did not want to get back in bed just yet. After swallowing her next dose of pain pills, Shannon began to feel groggy as she talked to Ben about the weather and the snow.

He carefully scooped her up out of the chair and into his arms, then set her on the bed, careful not to put any pressure on her incision site. Gently, he brought the covers up around her, tucking her in. "I can't believe you're Amelia's dad," Shannon said groggily. "Out of all the people in the world. I should have seen it coming," she mumbled.

Ben tried to shush her, but gave up as she continued rambling on. "Of course her dad is hot. Of course I banged her dad. This would happen to me... never going to work." As she began to fall fast asleep, Ben leaned down and kissed Shannon on her forehead, pushing her hair out of her face.

When the sun woke her up the next morning, Shannon looked down to see Ben on a chair next to her bed, fast asleep. His face was shadowed with an unshaven beard, and his mouth was open as he breathed quietly. She followed the trail of his arm to her bed, where she realized that his hand was enveloping hers. Just like Amelia, Shannon realized, she had a feeling that Ben was quickly becoming her best friend.

Amelia was able to go home later that day, and she dramatically said goodbye to Shannon, leaving her a coloring book and kids word search in case she got lonely. Shannon treasured the word search, and was so bored out of her mind that she actually completed it.

The doctor informed her that she was supposed to stay at the hospital for a few days more, and Shannon nearly cringed at the thought. What about the coffee shop? She was so relieved when her mother brought her a bag from home, including a comfortable cotton nightgown and her cell phone. Shannon was thrilled to find a text from Jorge who assured her that he had everything covered at the shop and recruited one of Jakob's sisters, Jodie, to help at the shop while Shannon was out.

Melissa told the cutest stories to Shannon about Jodie and so she knew everything was going to be fine. As much as the control freak in her wanted to jump out of the hospital bed, Shannon admittedly felt like crap. She was in a lot of pain from the surgery and the heavy antibiotics she was on were doing a number on her. She spent most of her hours sleeping and pretending that her life was not turning into one epic dumpster fire.

When the day finally came that the doctor cleared Shannon to go home, she was overjoyed as her father helped her climb into the back of his truck, her mother fussing around her and covering her up with a blanket. Once she was at home, her mother helped her take a shower, which was a humbling experience, and then she climbed into her bed and sipped on some homemade chicken and dumpling soup. She had to admit it—her mother was up there with Barb on the nurturing scale.

Her mother spent a few days with Shannon until

Shannon proved to her that she could shuffle about on her own. After her mother reluctantly left, shedding a few tears as she said goodbye to her headstrong daughter, Shannon binge-watched three seasons of *The Bachelorette* before throwing her remote across the room in disgust.

She was saved by Jorge, who came over in the middle of the day and practically gave Shannon a heart attack when she saw him. "Calm down, boss lady," Jorge said. "Jodie has it under control, seriously. She's a natural. Nothing phases that girl."

Shannon believed Jorge, having met Jodie a few times before. "I miss the shop so much. I want to come back. Maybe tomorrow," Shannon began.

"Yeah right," Jorge snorted. "You'll be out for another week, at the very least," he said. Jorge, while a dear friend, was not one for subtlety.

Shannon groaned at this. "So tell me about this rescue," Jorge said. "Did the hot cop really drive you to the hospital in a snowplow? You have no idea how badly I want him to be gay."

Shannon rolled her eyes. "I have no idea what he did or did not do," she said vaguely. "I was unconscious the entire time. Did you know that he's Amelia's dad?"

"Like adoptive dad or birth dad? Is there a husband?" Jorge asked inquisitively.

"Pretty sure there's a mom in the picture somewhere," Shannon said, realization hitting her for the first time that there *had* to be a mother in the picture. But where was she? Shannon hoped that there was not a mom at home waiting for Ben and Amelia. If Ben turned out to be a cheater, she would be crushed. It would ruin everything, especially her relationship with Amelia. She would be sick if she allowed herself to unknowingly become the other woman.

Telling Jorge that she was exhausted and needed to sleep, Shannon had a restless night's sleep as she thought about Ben and about Amelia's mother, wondering what in the world she got herself into, and how she was possibly going to get out of the situation.

Returning His Power

Chapter 11

The next day, Maddie and Melissa paid Shannon a long overdue visit. While at first the girls doted over Shannon, bringing her books and magazines to keep her company, the conversation quickly turned to the sisters' problems. Before long, Maddie and Melissa were both sobbing on Shannon's couch.

Maddie was crying about how much she missed Nick, convinced that his visa application would get rejected for one reason or another. That made Melissa begin to sob about the how the paint color in the nursery turned out too dark and how she did not want to offend Jakob by telling him that she hated it.

Shannon reached the end of her rope after twenty minutes of the girls and their literal sob stories. She pushed herself off the couch and stood in front of the sisters.

"That's it!" Shannon said sternly, her rose-colored matronly nightgown reaching the floor. "You guys are crying about things that aren't even real issues. Meanwhile, I am stuck in my house after almost dying and I might be sleeping with a married man. So, Maddie, calm down because you and I both know that everything is going to be fine with Nick. And Melissa, you go home and tell Jakob the truth. You know he would do anything for you. If you don't tell him you hate the color then I will."

The girls stared at Shannon with wide eyes as she went completely off the rails in front of them. Neither of them had any idea what man she was talking about, but they got the hint that Shannon *really* did not want to talk about it. The girls quickly dried up their sniffles and made a swift exit after giving Shannon hugs. As they pulled out of her driveway, Shannon went to the kitchen, slammed down a glass of water, and then went back to her couch to stew.

She was going absolutely nutty being cooped up like this. There were not enough old movies and crossword puzzles and books in the world to satisfy her. All she wanted to do was work at the coffee shop and be in a sexual relationship with someone who she knew for sure was single.

When her doorbell rang, Shannon let out a groan as she walked over to her front hall, dreading to have to sit through another visitor's sob stories.

She swung open the door and found Ben standing on her front porch, in jeans again, hands shoved in his pockets. "I wanted to text you to make sure I wasn't bothering you," Ben said, "but I didn't have your number. Then when I got halfway here, I realized it was probably on the paperwork you filled out at the station but I would have felt guilty using that in anything other than an official capacity and—"

Shannon cut him off from rambling any longer and said, tersely and to the point, "Are you married?"

"What?" Ben asked, his face contorting in confusion. "Am I married? God no, why?"

Shannon blew out a sigh of relief, then opened the door wider, gesturing for him to come in. "I was worried," Shannon said. "With Amelia, I got scared that you were married or with her mom."

Ben stopped taking off his boots to stand up and face her. "No, Shannon, it's not like that at all. I would never do that to you. Amelia has never even known her mother since the minute she was born." Shannon felt a mixture of relief and pain for Amelia at hearing this, a confusion of feelings overtaking her.

"It seems we have a lot to talk about," Ben said, slipping off his jacket. "Is now a good time?" He asked, eyeing her nightgown. "Please tell me I didn't wake you up."

Shannon shook her head as she walked into the living room, Ben following close behind her. "No, and even if you would have I wouldn't have minded. All I do is sleep these days."

"You need it," Ben said sweetly. "You're recovering from some pretty major stuff."

"Yeah," Shannon admitted. "That's true. I am just going crazy cooped up in this house."

"Understandable," Ben said. "I think I would

too."

The two sat in silence for some time, listening to the tick-tocking of Shannon's wall clock filling the void between them. Ben broke off the silence. "There's a lot I need to say to you," he began.

Shannon tucked her leg underneath her lap, careful to move gingerly. Ben sat on the chair across from her, pulling it closer. "I guess there's no better place to start than at the beginning," he mused.

Shannon nodded and waited for him to continue, taking a sip of water as she listened.

"I was born in Miami. My mom, Barb, went out there for college. She was studying to be a nurse, but really just wanted to escape Willow Falls and her strict family, to be anywhere but Wisconsin. She fell in love with the owner of a Cuban restaurant that she waitressed at on the weekends. Before long, she got pregnant with me. She was only twenty." Shannon nodded sympathetically at this, knowing plenty of young moms and understanding their struggles.

"When she told my father that she was pregnant, that was pretty much the end of the relationship. She lost her job at the restaurant, dropped out of college, and started working at a call center instead. She was too ashamed to come back home, and kept me a secret from her family for a long time. They are all gone now, but I guess they were some real pieces of work.

I grew up in Miami. Mom worked long hours but always made sure that I was provided for. She never fell in love again, it was just me and her taking on the world. Once I was older, she eventually took night classes and became a court stenographer. When I graduated high school, I knew I wanted to join the police academy. We didn't grow up in the best neighborhood and I wanted to change things for kids like me, to clean up the streets.

I went through the academy and got a job with Miami PD. I was working for about five years with the best partner a guy could have. Mark was a great guy, funny as hell, always had my back. He was shot one night during a drug deal gone bad and died on the operating table later that day. It was my night off." Ben shook his head at the memory, as if trying to get it out of his head.

"I'll never forgive myself for not being there for him. That same night, Amelia was born. I was at the hospital two floors away from my best friend. When Amelia came into this world, Mark was leaving it, and I had no idea."

A tear fell out of the corner of Shannon's eye as she listened to Ben tell his story. "Amelia's mother, she was never anything serious. We met at a cop bar, and it was always casual with her. We had a good time together, nothing else. When she got pregnant, I knew I needed to step it up and be the father that I never had. She didn't have the same feelings about being a mother, though. She wanted to travel the world, to not have anything tie her down.

I don't know how anybody could look at Amelia after she was born and sign away the rights to her, but Mickey did just that, and it's been just Amelia and I— and my amazing mom—ever since. We haven't heard from her, and for Amelia's sake, I hope it stays that way."

"Wow," Shannon said, absolutely stunned at all

of Ben's revelations. There was so much more to him than she thought. Of course, she knew that Ben was a person with a lot of depth and a lot of heart, but she could have never imagined that such tragedy and pain was behind those blue eyes of his. "I am so sorry about all of this—about your partner, about Amelia's mother. I can't believe it. It's all so sad. But she is so very lucky to have you and to have Barb."

"And you," Ben said. "She idolizes you." Shannon's head about exploded when Ben said that.

"No," she insisted. "I am the wrong person for her to idolize. I am pretty messed up in my own ways."

"I disagree," Ben said. "In fact, if I had to say, I'd guess you're pretty close to perfect," he said, leaning over and clutching her hand.

Tears streamed down Shannon's face as she looked at him, then pulled her hand away from him. "No," Shannon said. "I can't do this with you. I just can't."

Hurt covered Ben's face as he looked at Shannon, imploring her to explain further. Hearing nothing from her, he stood up. "You're just tired and you've been through a lot. We can talk about this another day," he said.

"No," Shannon said adamantly. "There's nothing else to say," she said, sitting back in the couch.

Ben looked at Shannon, staring blankly at her. Then he nodded curtly and bent down, kissing her on the forehead before walking out of her house and, Shannon figured, out of her life forever.

There was nothing she could do or say to justify why she was lashing out the way that she was. There was nothing to be done about what was already said and what was not yet said.

Finding herself sobbing on her couch just like Maddie and Melissa were not too long ago, Shannon pulled herself off of the couch and marched upstairs, resigning herself to bed until she could snap out of whatever fit of emotions were currently taking over her body.

Returning His Power

Chapter 12

A few days later—but probably still more early than was healthy—Shannon went back to work. She toned down her outfits, and instead wore cozy patterned leggings and tunics. Jorge was thrilled to see her again, but it was very clear that Jodie really did have a natural talent for working in the coffee shop.

Even though Shannon was back, she asked Jodie to stay on, realizing that the extra help was a huge relief for both her and Jorge. Jodie was bubbly, funny, and always willing to go the extra mile. Although she was young, she had spunk and Shannon was happy to have her on the team.

A lot of her regulars were glad to see Shannon back, curious about where she was. They had heard rumors that she was in the hospital, but most of the townspeople were smarter than to believe everything they heard in Willow Falls. When they realized that the rumor about the new police chief rescuing Shannon in a snowplow was true, everyone was practically skipping down the icy sidewalks in excitement with a new story to share.

Maddie and Melissa came into the coffeeshop with a huge bouquet of flowers, apologizing for their outburst. Shannon apologized, too, and the girls all hugged it out.

"So, kind of exciting," Maddie began. "The visa process got moved forward another step!" she revealed quickly. Shannon and Maddie stood and squealed in the middle of the coffee shop as Melissa sat back and laughed at the two.

"And the paint color?" Shannon asked Melissa eagerly.

"Jakob repainted it on Monday," Melissa said. "I am so embarrassed that I freaked out about something so unimportant in the scheme of things."

Shannon shrugged it off, "It's probably the hormones," she said. "Mark my words, you're having a girl."

"How can you be so sure?" Maddie asked skeptically.

"I just know," Shannon said matter-of-factly. "Don't question such things," she said with a smile as she poured Maddie a coffee and Melissa a decaf tea.

"Another reason we stopped by," Melissa said, stepping closer to the counter. "It was about what you told us," she murmured. "About the guy. Do you need to talk?" she asked, concern in her voice.

"Oh, *phshh*," Shannon replied, waving them off. "No. Crisis averted. Not married."

Melissa clutched her chest in relief.

"But still," Maddie said. "That's not really going to be enough details for me. Considering that my fiancé is currently 3,500 miles away, I think I at least should get the details about who is fucking who."

"Who is fucking Shannon?" Jorge asked, sliding up to Shannon's side, leaning his elbows on the counter, head balancing on his palms.

"Nobody is fucking anybody," Shannon said quietly as she stormed into the kitchen, baking a batch of cookies instead of immersing herself in more gossip.

The days went by faster now that Shannon was back in her element. On Friday, Shannon walked into work in a pair of hot pink leggings and a black shirt that read, "This is what a feminist looks like." She swooped her hair up in a baseball cap and began getting muffins and scones baked for the day.

Jodie came in before Jorge, bringing along a crate of butter from her family's farm. Jodie had her long dark brown hair woven in two thick braids. She wore a plain blue dress, and took off her cap when she removed her jacket. She eagerly placed one of the baseball hats on her head and tied a black apron around her waist.

Jodie worked diligently getting all the coffee machines ready for the morning brews, then assisting Shannon with frosting a batch of cookies. When Shannon began to get worn out, Jodie insisted that Shannon go in her office and do some computer work while she take over to handle the morning crowd with

Jorge.

Shannon was glad for the break. She ended up spending the majority of the day in her office catching up on orders and paperwork. She paid a pile of outstanding bills and soon the piles and piles of paperwork on her desk began to dwindle.

With a sigh, she stood up and stretched, then went out to check on the cafe. After grabbing a scone and a cup of coffee, she went back to her office, placing some orders and looking over the prints for the work that needed to be done in her addition.

She was behind schedule because of her surgery, but Shannon was confident that she could get back on track. She reminded herself to call her brothers to see when they would be able to come and help her get the kitchen renovation started.

Shannon was just about getting double-vision from staring at the computer screen for too long when she heard a familiar laugh. Poking her head out of the office, her face lit up as she saw Amelia standing at the counter with Barb, laughing at something Jorge said to her.

Before she could stop herself, Shannon ran out and hugged Amelia, who was overjoyed to see her. "I have missed you so much, Shannon!" Amelia squealed as Shannon embraced the child.

"I missed you too, honey," Shannon said. Her heartstrings tore as she thought about everything that happened with Amelia's dad, and the reasons why she acted the way she did.

"How are you feeling? How's life without tonsils?" Shannon asked, breaking the embrace to take a good look at Amelia.

"I feel so much better," Amelia said. "And look," she said, pointing to her mouth, "I lost another tooth." Amelia grinned toothlessly for Shannon and she made sure to appear especially impressed.

"Well look at you!" Shannon said. "Did the tooth fairy come?"

"Mmhmm," Amelia said. "I got five dollars under my pillow. But Shannon?" Amelia said, leaning in closer to her.

"Yeah?" Shannon asked, responding to the little girl.

"Since we are best friends, I feel like I need to tell you that the tooth fairy isn't really a fairy at all. It's my dad."

Shannon pretended to look surprised at Amelia's revelation. "What?" Shannon asked dramatically, putting her hand on her chest. "Are you sure?"

Amelia nodded knowingly. "I saw him with my own eyes when he thought I was sleeping. So next time you lose a tooth, it's really my dad that sneaks into your bedroom."

Shannon nearly snorted at Amelia's choice of wording, then nodded solemnly. "Good to know," she said, standing up to greet Barb.

"How are you honey?" Barb asked her, pulling her into a tight hug.

"I'm doing well," Shannon said.

"Oh good," Barb said. "I feel like we have all been missing you, Amelia for sure. And Ben has been coming home from work so tired lately. He hasn't been coming back early in the morning with those cute travel mugs that you give out your coffee in. It must not have tasted the same without you here," she said, knowing exactly what she was saying but not needing to spell it out.

Shannon blushed as she realized that Barb knew the entire time that something was up with her and Ben, and the thought that Barb guessed that the two spent nights together made her more mortified than she had been in a long time.

The cross-connection between the two very polarized parts of Shannon's world still made her head spin if she thought about it too hard.

After saying goodbye to Barb and Amelia, Shannon stepped into the new addition for the first time since returning to work. She nearly fell backwards as she stared at a brand new, state-of-the-art kitchen. "Oh my god," she whispered to herself as she walked over, rubbing her hand along the stainless steel surfaces and the brand new countertops.

It was everything from her plans, like she was stepping into her dreams for the first time. Even the state-of-the-art refrigerator that she spent hours pining over was there. She shook her head in disbelief at the talented work, knowing that three very special men in her life—four with her father—were responsible for this work.

Pulling out her cell phone, she dialed her dad's number and he answered quickly, "So you finally saw it, eh kid?" he asked with a laugh.

"Dad!" Shannon said with a screech. "It's perfect, better than my wildest dreams. How did you possibly get all this done?"

"The boys finished up the auditorium project early with all those days the kids were out of school. We had some time while you were recovering and were able to get it done. Anything for our favorite girl."

"You and I both know that Mom is your favorite girl so don't even pretend," Shannon said with a laugh. She could see the laugh lines on her father's face as he chuckled into the phone.

"I love you, kid," her dad said. "You've got four men who love you no matter what."

Shannon smiled as she listened to her father's kind words.

After thanking him again and promising to come to family dinner soon, Shannon hung up and stared in amazement at the kitchen, hardly believing that the oven and stovetop were really hers, that the eclectic blue tiling that she picked out covered the floor, and that everything was moving so fast.

The sunlight began to fall as Shannon hung up a few light pieces of artwork on the walls of the new addition. With every piece that she hung, it began to feel more and more like the cozy coffee shop that she knew and loved.

Soon, Jorge closed up the shop and she was all alone, promising not to stay too much longer. Shannon took a step back from the painting that she hung up, looked at it satisfactorily, then walked to other room to get her jacket and head home. She caught a glimpse of headlights out the window.

The police cruiser slowed in front of the coffee shop. Shannon's heart caught as she watched the truck slow down, waiting for it to stop. Instead, the cruiser continued driving past.

Shannon would be lying to herself if she did not admit that she was disappointed. There was so much she wanted to say to Ben, so many things she wanted to share but she was scared of what he would think of her.

As she walked out to her car, Shannon breathed in the cold winter air. She had a feeling that, as messed up as things were, she was going to be okay. She was gaining more and more strength each and every day and would be much better in time.

When she woke up the next morning, Shannon hardly expected to have ten missed calls and five voicemails. Her heart beat fast as she began to listen, seeing that Maddie and Melissa both called, worried that something terrible had happened.

When the two both screamed into the phone with joy, Shannon felt immediate relief. She was even more surprised when they told her that Carlson was kicked off the Village Board last night.

She speed-dialed Margaret as she made a pot of coffee, her bob royally messed up with bedhead.

"Good morning, champion," Margaret said, the smile in her face evident as she answered the phone.

"What happened?" Shannon asked, confused at Margaret's words.

"The Board met last night. I had Hazel from down the street drive me. Everything was going along normally until the Board all turned to Carlson and confronted him about the emails he sent. He really had no defense. The proof is in the pudding. They offered him the chance to resign gracefully. He refused, so they voted unanimously to kick him off the Board!"

"Holy shit!" Shannon said. It was hard for her to believe that she had a part in finally taking down a corrupt leader. "What did he do?"

"He stormed out of the meeting room. He was so embarrassed," Margaret said. "You made this happen, kid," she said proudly.

Shannon sat on her couch, hardly believing that this was real life. She was so proud of the Board for standing up for what was right. But their fight was not over. She still needed to ensure that Carlson began treating his employees with dignity and legally. She made a mental note to call her friend Holly and check in on what the ACLU had to say about everything going on.

After finishing her conversation with Margaret, Shannon took a long shower before figuring out what to wear for the day. Feeling physically better than she had for days, she decided to slip on a red wine hued velvet wrap dress that went down to her midthighs with a pair of black tights. As Shannon brushed glitter eyeshadow on, she smiled at herself in the mirror. Even dressing in her favorite outfits made her feel better, always able to express herself through fashion.

When she walked into the coffee shop that morning, Jorge and Jodie were busily preparing to open the shop, but they stopped and stared when Shannon took off her white faux fur cape.

"What?" Shannon asked casually.

"She's back!" Jorge said with a smile, handing Shannon a shot of espresso.

With a laugh, Shannon swallowed the drink then got busy counting the till. It was going to be a good day.

When the morning paper hit the front door, it

was Shannon's cue to unlock the coffee shop and turn on all the lights. As she made her way through the shop, turning on all of her little quirky lamps, she smiled at the rising sun. Even the sun was celebrating the victory.

She opened the front door of the shop and bent down to pick up the paper. Her dark blue eyes grew wide as she read the headlines, "Carlson impeached from Willow Falls Board, Retires as CEO of Carlson Canning." She quickly scanned the article, reading that he retired yesterday, effective immediately, and that his son was going to take over. "I plan on working with the newly formed union to make some changes and keep up with the times," his son was quoted as saying.

Jumping up and down with delight, Shannon ran back inside the coffee shop and showed Jorge the article, who hugged her for about three minutes straight. She went in her office to call Holly, who was over the moon excited about the new union. She said that she heard that a lot of former employees were even thinking about coming back with the old regime out and new union rules in effect. Shannon promised to come to their first meeting to see what was happening and show her support, then let Holly go so she could continue working with the ACLU.

Shannon knew this called for a celebration of epic proportions. After going home for family dinner tonight, she planned to figure out something she could do to celebrate the victory.

Shannon's mother was ecstatic when she heard the news, but scolded Shannon for laying down in the middle of the street. "What would have stopped those trucks from running you right over?" Celeste exclaimed as she poured sauce over her stuffed shells. "You could have died, again!" she said.

"They would not have run me over, Ma, that's the point," Shannon said as she sipped coffee at her mom's counter.

"You do realize that your father knows about this, don't you?" Celeste said, stopping her cooking to look at Shannon from above her bifocals.

"And?" Shannon said. "I am almost thirty years old."

"Try telling that to Dad," Celeste said with a smile.

Shannon sighed as she took another sip, then smiled as her father walked in the kitchen, a green Romano Construction shirt on with a pair of well-worn jeans. "There's my baby girl!" Phil Senior said to Shannon, wrapping her up in his arms.

"Aren't you retired?" Shannon asked, gesturing at his shirt.

He shrugged, his salt and pepper beard glimmering in the kitchen lights. "Just helping the boys out a bit when I can," her dad sad sheepishly.

"You better take it easy, mister!" Shannon said to him.

"This is coming from the woman who singlehandedly took down that sorry excuse for a man Carlson while she had an appendix bursting inside of her," her dad said. "I don't always agree with the things you do and the decisions you make, but I am really proud of you, kid," he said, placing a hand on Shannon's shoulder.

Shannon's heart warmed to hear her father's

praise. She really admired her father and took what he said seriously. She knew that her wild antics worried her parents, but they were pretty used to her extravagant behavior by now.

After a nice dinner with her family, Shannon went home and scoured the internet for local events, looking for something that would be the perfect fit for her celebration outing. Clicking on a link, Shannon nodded her head. She had the *perfect* idea.

Chapter 13

After a delicious steak dinner along the river in Milwaukee, Shannon drove to one of her favorite places on earth, Cinema 62 on the east side of the city. To go into the theater was to step into a time capsule of years past. The movie theater played nothing but classic films. As she walked up to the theater, she enjoyed the 1950s architecture, with lime green lights and art deco design.

"Singin' in the Rain" was lit up on the sign. There was only one screen in the small theater, but it was perfect. Shannon bought her ticket, then bought a container of popcorn and a soda. She walked into the dark theater and found her favorite seat on the end of the row towards the front. She sipped her soda as she watched the old previews, munching on the buttery popcorn.

When the film began, she allowed herself to get immersed in the musical as if she was viewing it for the first time instead of the fiftieth. She hummed along with the songs, captivated by Gene Kelly's suave dance moves.

The musical was nearly over when the soda hit Shannon hard. She snuck out the theater and used the restroom. As she was walking out the bathroom, Ben was walking out of the men's room. They stood there, in the doorways of the bathroom, for longer than was probably necessary, and just stared at each other.

"Shannon," Ben said quietly.

"Hey, Officer," she said to him, a smile on her face as she saw the man that she hated to admit that she had missed. They stepped out into the quiet hallway, getting closer to each other. "Are you here with Amelia?" Shannon asked, smiling even more as she thought about her little buddy watching *Singin' in the Rain*.

"Yes," Ben said. "Amelia's latest crush is Gene Kelly and I don't have the heart to tell her that—even if he was still alive—he'd be way too old for her," he continued with a smile.

Shannon bit her lip as she laughed, thinking about Amelia going googly-eyed over the actor. "We all go through a Gene Kelly phase," she told him. "I don't think mine ever went away, though."

"But you got over your Ben phase pretty quickly, huh?" Ben said to her, his white smile disappearing as his blue eyes pierced her soul.

"Not even a little bit," Shannon said to him quietly. "There's so much I want to say to you, but I don't know how to say it," she admitted.

"You can tell me anything, Shannon," Ben said.

"I am so freaking damaged, Ben," she admitted. "You deserve to be with someone who has her life together, who knows what she wants. I don't think I am meant to settle down."

"Do you really think you don't have your life together?" Ben said, getting angry now. "That's the most ridiculous thing I ever heard and you know it," he said, stepping forward, his muscled body taking up the space, making Shannon suck in a breath and hold it tight.

"I don't know," Shannon said, not feeling confident at all about her admission.

"And as far as being damaged. Well, we all are, but when I was with you, it made me forget about everything even if just for a bit, about all of the mistakes I've made, about the things that I wish I would have done differently."

Shannon broke eye contact with him as she thought about it, realizing that she felt the same way. When she was with him, nothing else mattered. Real life went out the window and instead she was able to just focus on Ben, on being happy.

"Look at me," Ben said quietly but sternly. When Shannon looked up at him, he reached forward, cupping her chin.

"I'm begging you to open up to me," Ben said. "Please."

Shannon nodded, leaning into Ben's warm body. "I promise." He pulled her into his arms, his strong hold sweeping her up, making her feel protected. If Shannon was to admit it, she would say that she never felt anything better than being enveloped in his arms, caught up in the electric sparks that emanated between their bodies.

Ben leaned down, his big hands cupping Shannon's cheeks. He nodded at Shannon and she nodded back. Ben darted down, slowly, but deliberately, and kissed Shannon with everything he had in his soul, wanting nothing more than to connect with her.

Ben's mouth felt electric against her own, as if his kiss was a necessary means to recharge her heart. He pressed her against the wall, gently and protectively, as they deepened the kiss, taking things further and further.

Shannon forgot where she was, forgot that she and Ben were not the only two people in the world. The kiss completely and totally captivated her, making her crave for more. She wanted to touch him, for him to touch her, to feel him inside of her.

She nearly jumped out of her skin as she heard a gasp and then a tiny voice shout, "Miss Shannon!" Ben tore away from her as they both stared down at the source of the voice. Amelia was standing in front of them, feather boa in tow, her mouth wide open in shock. Barb stood behind Amelia with a grin from ear to ear.

"Amelia—," Ben and Shannon both said at the same time.

"I knew it," Amelia said smartly. "I knew you liked each other," she said proudly, as if she just tapped in the last piece of a puzzle.

Ben looked at Shannon, then down at Amelia, his face redder than ever. He ran a hand through his hair, then bent down to look at Amelia eye-to-eye. "Amelia, Shannon and I are really good friends," he began to explain, clunkily and unsure.

"Good friends who like to smooch!" Amelia retorted with a giggle, stuffing her hand in her box of popcorn and shoving a handful in her mouth as Barb snickered quietly.

"Something like that," Ben said, clearly defeated by his six-year-old and at a complete loss for words.

"Since you two are friends and Shannon's my best friend, maybe she should come to pizza night tomorrow?" Amelia asked her father slyly, her doe eyes imploring as she stared up at him.

"That's completely up to her," Ben said, looking up at Shannon.

There was absolutely no way that Shannon could resist her little buddy's request, and she quickly nodded in agreement.

People began filing out of the theater and, after solidifying plans for five o'clock the next night, Shannon walked to the parking lot with them. She watched Ben carefully lift Amelia up into the backseat of his truck, taking time to fasten her seatbelt, then press a kiss on her forehead.

She smiled as she drove out of the parking lot, headed towards the freeway to make it back to Willow Falls. There was hope that she could heal, that she could tell Ben everything, that things were really beginning to look up.

The next evening, Ben paced around his historic two story home, trying yet failing to ignore Amelia's dramatic wails as she threw her clothes around her bedroom, not knowing what to wear, and Barb's shouts from the kitchen about overflowing the coffeepot.

He wore an unbuttoned green and black flannel

shirt with a black long sleeve thermal shirt underneath, fitting against his muscular abs. His dark wash jeans were hardly broken in, as he was usually in his uniform pants.

Amelia ran down the stairs, a pink tutu on and strings of pearls around her neck. Marching into the kitchen, Ben watched as Barb sponged up coffee from the counter and the floor. He wanted to pull his hair out as he watched the disaster unfold. Amelia came running into the kitchen. Ben instinctively threw his arm out, blocking Amelia from running right into the puddle of coffee. Sweeping her up in his arms, she laughed as he carried her to the living room just as the doorbell rang.

Shannon stood outside on their front wraparound porch, chilly in the cold air. She held an apple pie in both hands, hoping that Amelia would like it. Ben swung open the door, an elated Amelia sitting in his arms. They greeted Shannon warmly, a smile breaking out on Ben's face when he saw her.

Shannon slipped off her jacket to reveal a t-shirt that said, "Women belong in the house and the senate" underneath a chunky knit pink cardigan. She wore a comfortable pair of black leggings on the bottom. As she hung up her jacket on the hook, Amelia cautiously held the pie. Ben set her down and told her to take it into the kitchen with *walking feet*, hoping that Barb cleaned up the coffee disaster.

They stood in his front hall for some time, just looking at each other. Shannon could not deny how attractive Ben looked in his casual attire, so different from his typical formal look in his uniform. She liked the way he looked at home, relaxed and at ease.

"You look great," Ben said, as if reading her mind. She looked down at her t-shirt, leggings, and fuzzy socks. "Not nearly as great as you do," Shannon said, reaching up and catching his dimple between her two fingers.

Ben smiled as she touched him, the electric spark back again. Barb walked out of the kitchen, rubbing her hands on a towel. "Shannon!" she exclaimed excitedly. "We are so glad you could come. Please, come on in and make yourself at home," she pleaded.

Shannon smiled as she walked into the cozy home and as Barb gave her a hug. Barb was wearing a pair of jeans and a blue sweatshirt that said "#1 Grandma" on the front.

Amelia grabbed Shannon's hand and led her into the living room, a cute room that had built-in bookshelves on three of the walls. A big oversized couch was perched in front of the windows. "Let me give you a tour, darling," Amelia said. She led Shannon through their home, pointing out her favorite places and spots. Shannon just loved their house. As she followed Amelia upstairs, she swallowed as she thought about seeing Ben's bedroom.

Amelia pushed open the first door at the top of the stairs. Pale pink paint covered the walls as she stepped into the room. A big queen size bed with a luxurious cream-colored headboard and footboard nearly filled the entire room. Framed movie posters and photographs of classic movie stars—Audrey Hepburn, Judy Garland, Vivien Leigh—filled the walls. Amelia walked towards an antique vanity and sat down at the stool.

"Daddy got this for me," she said proudly, peering into the mirror and grabbing a tube of chapstick, applying it delicately as if she were putting on ruby red lipstick.

"It's so cool," Shannon said, rubbing her hand along the wood detailing.

"He's the best," Amelia said. "I'm so glad you are friends, too." Amelia stood up then walked to the door. "I'll show you his room, then we can go downstairs and eat pizza."

Shannon had to admit that she was excited to see what Ben's bedroom looked like. Her nosy self was itching with anticipation as they made their way down the hallway.

Amelia pushed open the door at the end of the stairs. Shannon was enveloped with the scent of Ben. She walked into the room gingerly, taking in the king size bed that was covered by a maroon comforter. The bed was neatly made, a pine headboard adding masculinity to the room. The room was small, yet comfortable. A big overstuffed chair was in the corner, a pile of books on the table next to it.

She walked towards his nightstand and saw a kid-friendly cookbook on it, pieces of scrap paper marking pages. She smiled at this. *Fuck*, Ben was cute.

She looked down at Amelia and grinned, then let the little girl lead her back downstairs. "Grandma lives above the garage," she explained. "She has her whole own apartment. Daddy says she deserves her space sometimes because we can be overwhelming." Shannon had to laugh at this. Barb certainly did deserve her own space.

When they walked in the kitchen, Ben was standing nervously in front of the fridge, a cup of coffee in his hands.

"Oh, Shannon," Barb said. "I made you some coffee. Would you like a cup?" she asked eagerly.

"I'd love one, thank you," Shannon said, walking in and sitting down at the breakfast nook. Barb filled a cup full of coffee then set it down in front of her.

"It smells delicious," Shannon said, putting the cup up to her lips to take a sip. As she tasted the coffee, she caught some coffee grounds between her lips and reluctantly swallowed the thick sludge. She cleared her throat, unable to hold back a cough. "Oh wow," Shannon said, urging herself to be polite. "It tastes great," she choked out.

Barb clutched her hands in excitement. "That means so much coming from the coffee queen herself!"

Shannon looked at Amelia and Ben who stood in front of her, traumatized. Ben shook his head in apology and Amelia grimaced, waving her hand in front of her neck, fervently making the no go gesture.

Shannon silently laughed at the two of them, obsessed with how cute they were together. Barb sat down next to Shannon and Amelia climbed into the breakfast booth as well. They began talking about school and the snow and how much they liked it here.

The doorbell rang shortly after and Ben came back into the kitchen carrying pizza boxes. He set them in the middle of the table and grabbed some plates from the cupboard. He went to the fridge and brought some cans of soda over to the table, setting one in front of Shannon. She looked up at him gratefully as she pushed her coffee cup aside.

They enjoyed their pizza. The majority of their dinner conversation revolved around Amelia, who told everyone stories of art class and recess and going sledding for the first time.

After they finished their pizza, Amelia went into the living room to turn on Turner Classic Movies. "Hey Amelia," Ben called from the kitchen. "Do you think you can come in here and help Grandma load the dishwasher."

"Oh sorry, darling," she called back from the living room. "I just can't. Ever since my procedure I just haven't been the same. So sorry, darling," she said sweetly.

Shannon laughed. "Sounds like Scarlett O'Hara is having a rough day," she said to Ben and Barb as she carried her plate over to the sink.

"She seems to have lots of them lately, especially when she needs to help with chores," Barb said, laughing at her granddaughter.

Barb shooed the two out of the kitchen and they went into the living room. Shannon sat on the comfortable couch, snuggling into the pillows. Amelia was laying on the floor, enthralled with the television. Ben sat down next to Shannon, careful to keep his distance between her.

As they watched the movie, Shannon reached out to take Ben's hand in hers, giving it a quick squeeze then letting go. Ben looked over at her and smiled, catching her hand and squeezing it in return.

Chapter 14

It was the perfect evening, Shannon decided. Barb served them all the apple pie and they spent the evening chatting and watching television. Barb went to bed early, leaving to go to her apartment above the garage. Amelia was sound asleep on the floor by nine o'clock. Instead of waking her, Ben bent down and swept her up gently in his arms, quietly carrying her up the stairs. Amelia mumbled something about needing to be on set in ten minutes before dropping her head on Ben's shoulder.

After tucking her in, Ben walked back downstairs, finding Shannon still cuddled up on the couch. He reached to the back of the couch and picked up a deep blue chunky knit blanket. "Barb isn't much of a cook, or a coffee expert, but she does know how to knit," he said, draping the blanket over Shannon's legs.

She huddled under the soft blanket, pulling it up around her body. "This is amazing," she said. "So cozy."

"For sure," Ben said, sitting next to her on the couch, his hand on her knee.

"Please hear me out," Shannon said.

"Take your time," Ben said, really meaning it. His eyes roamed over her face, not wanting to miss a moment.

"I was married before," Shannon burst out. Ben's eyes grew wide at her admission, not expecting her to say that. "I was eighteen years old, living in Milwaukee and going to college. We met in an accounting class. He was a senior and already had a job lined up after graduation. Things seemed to be perfect with him. He was everything that girls are told to look for in a guy: respectful, responsible, a provider. I thought I was doing the right thing by getting married to him," she explained.

Ben patted her knee supportively, silently encouraging her that she was safe to talk about anything with him.

"I quickly realized that I was delusional. After we got married, everything became about having children. He wanted me to drop out and get pregnant right after the wedding. Kids were something we talked about down the line but I wanted to finish college first.

That wasn't good enough for him, though. He wanted to come home from work everyday with dinner on the table and he wanted kids immediately. It wasn't going to work. I filed for divorce during finals week of my freshman year. We were divorced two months later."

"That's a shame," Ben said sympathetically. "But I'm really glad that you were able to get out before getting trapped in something you didn't want."

"That's very true," Shannon said. "I am definitely lucky in that regard. But, in some way, those six months that we were married was too long. It was long enough for me to realize that it is not a situation I ever want to find myself in again."

"That's completely understandable," Ben replied. "But does that mean that you are going to cut yourself off from every chance at love?"

"Not intentionally," Shannon admitted. "I am just terrified to get hurt again, to feel like I am not enough."

Ben nodded, but refused to accept Shannon's answer. He leaned forward, tucking her hair behind her ear. "Shannon, don't you see what you're worth? Don't you know that any man would be so lucky to have you as his own?"

Shannon looked up at Ben, her gray eyeshadow making her dark eyes even more pronounced in the dim light of the room. "But it's not about them," Shannon insisted. "It's about me. It's about how I need room to be free and make my own decisions and not let anybody ever tell me what to do. How can a man promise to do all those things? I wouldn't expect anyone to be able to do that, which is why I am better off alone."

"That's bullshit," Ben said. "You need someone who gives you room to do all those things, to know that you're smart enough to make the right decisions, to be waiting for you when you're ready for him," he pleaded.

Shannon thought about it for a moment. "It's not fair to you," she said, "for me to string you along like this. I don't know what I want anymore. I am so confused. With Amelia in the picture, it makes everything so much more serious. I don't want to come into her life and be around her like this if I don't know for sure that I'm going to stick around. She doesn't need anybody else leaving her. But to be honest with you, I don't know if I can do it. I don't know if I can be the mother figure she needs. I've never been the maternal type." Shannon was out of breath by the time she sped through everything she was thinking, dumping all of her fears and concerns onto Ben.

Ben sat up, leaning forward and rubbing Shannon's cheek with the rough skin of his thumb. His eyes darted around her face, pondering what he could possibly say to Shannon to make her understand just how special she was.

"After everything that went down with Amelia's mom, I made sure to protect her from ever getting hurt like that again. I tried to wrap her in bubble wrap and protect her from getting attached to someone only to have them leave. When she first told me about you, I don't know what I was picturing but it wasn't you. When she described you, I figured you were a nice little old lady who also liked classic movies and baking cookies. You're nothing like what I thought, and if I would have known that you are this gorgeous single woman, I probably would have tried to keep her away from you, because I would undoubtedly fall for you and mess it up.

Amelia fell for you fast and so did I. You're such an amazing person. I know that, no matter what happens between us, nothing would affect your friendship with Amelia. The thought never even crossed my mind. You don't realize how great you are. You don't have to want to birth a bunch of kids to be motherly. You don't have to stop fighting for what's right to be motherly. You just have to keep being yourself," Ben said.

Shannon nodded, tears streaming down her face. Ben leaned in and kissed them away from her cheeks. "But the most important thing that you need to know is that everything that happens is up to you. You need to feel comfortable with your decision, and I will support you with whatever you decide, even if that means you and I not giving this a shot."

She was floored by his kindness and by Ben's complete and total respect for her autonomy. Never in her life had she encountered a man so willing to entrust a female with decision-making, with knowing that she would do the right thing both for herself and others.

Shannon swept the tears away from her face. She sat quietly for a few moments, just looking at Ben. His hair was messy and he had a crumb of apple pie on his shirt. She smiled as she picked it off, then leaned in closer to him. "Let's give it a shot," she whispered.

His face absolutely lit up as he heard her words. "Yeah?" he asked her, excitement in his voice.

"Definitely," Shannon said, giggling as he dove in to kiss her.

It was late when Shannon tiptoed out of the house and to her car. Ben followed her to her car, opening her door for her and making sure she got in safely. He leaned down to give her one last kiss, lingering as she clutched his bottom lip between her teeth, saucily teasing him.

She was happy. So, so happy. She was also

terrified, but feeling such excitement for the first time in a long time beat out any feelings of terror.

When she stepped into the coffee shop the next morning, Jorge immediately knew something was up. "Did someone replace the piss in your Cheerios with vodka?" he asked her sarcastically, viewing her wide smile skeptically. Then, he snapped his fingers and pointed at her. "You got laid!" He said, proud of his deduction.

Jodie looked over at them, blushing and giggling as she steamed milk.

"Nobody got laid!" Shannon said adamantly, then apologizing to Jodie for the outburst.

"You keep saying that," Jorge said. "And I am not so sure I believe it," he replied, walking into the kitchen as the oven timer went off.

Nothing could get Shannon down. She was planning a trip to Milwaukee with Melissa and Maddie to pick out more tables and chairs for the new addition, and they would begin transitioning to using the full service kitchen for everyday coffee service.

She needed to find someone to become the breakfast chef but unfortunately was not coming up with any good leads.

When the girls got together to head out shopping, Maddie pulled up in front of the coffee shop with her SUV. Melissa was sitting in the front seat, clutching her little baby belly proudly.

Shannon climbed in the back, quickly catching up on all the gossip. Jakob had kindly agreed to meet them with a trailer after they were done shopping to haul their purchases back to the coffee shop.

Maddie chattered on and on about Nick and the puppy that he got her. She was busy as ever potty training the puppy and working on a proposal for a full time teen librarian, doing anything she could to keep busy and stop worrying about the visa application.

Melissa casually brought up that a baby supply warehouse was only ten minutes away from the salvage mall that they were going to. Shannon and Maddie looked at each other and promised Melissa that they would be sure to make a stop. Melissa's face lit up and she clutched her belly, perhaps the most eager expectant mother to ever exist.

Shannon couldn't help but wonder what it must feel like to be so excited to have a baby, to want a child more than anything else in the world. She doubted that she would ever feel that way, and felt a little sad at the thought.

Tossing the subject out of her mind, she absorbed herself in girl talk instead, trying to remain present instead of getting lost in her thoughts.

The girls scored big at the salvage mall, finding more than enough quirky tables and chairs to fill up the shop. Shannon nearly screamed when she came upon a gorgeous set of wooden booths with tables, knowing she needed them for up against her front windows.

Jakob walked into the salvage shop, eyeing up Shannon's purchases. When he looked at the booths that Shannon bought, his eyes grew wide. Looking at Maddie, he said, "I don't suppose you can tell that fiancé of yours to hurry up and get here so he can help me haul this stuff, can you?"

Maddie laughed. "I'll tell him to make it snappy."

Jakob urged the girls to go to lunch while he finished packing everything up, telling them he would meet them back in Willow Falls. He gave Melissa a long kiss before he said goodbye, lovingly touching her stomach.

After enjoying lunch at a local salad place, the girls drove to the baby supply warehouse. Melissa filled a cart with things, *oohing* and *ahhing* at every new thing that she saw. Shannon was carrying a baby tub filled with pacifiers and bottles to the car when Maddie said, "Shannon, I have to admit, you looked pretty excited in there."

Shannon scoffed at this. "Strictly in an auntie, capacity, Madeline Danzer," she said. "Just like you, right?"

Maddie laughed. "Nick and I have already talked about it. We don't think kids are in the future but we are very excited about being an aunt and uncle."

Shannon nodded positively at this. She was glad that Maddie seemed to have everything figured out. She wished that she would have been more thoughtful about such things in the past. It would have saved her a lot of heartache, she mused.

When they got back to Willow Falls, her brother Marco was helping Jakob unload the furniture into the coffee shop. Shannon got excited as she saw it beginning to pile up in the addition. She began moving it over the wooden floors—which her brothers also refinished when she was out of commission—and arranging the tables and chairs in a way that made most sense to her.

The guys set up the booths in front of the big front windows and Shannon stood back and smiled.

This was it. This was what she was working so hard for, for a perfectly cozy space with good people and good coffee.

After giving Jakob and Marco two big hugs for their help, Shannon spent the evening with Melissa and Maddie, bringing out decor that she had been saving up in storage. They listened to soft R 'n' B as they plugged in lamps and arranged faux foliage around the shop.

Before they knew it, they were laughing late into the night, having the best time just spending it with each other. Although they had not been friends forever, Shannon certainly felt as if they were old friends and she trusted them with her heart. Which was exactly why, after clearing her throat and turning down the music, Shannon decided to tell them everything—all about Ben and Amelia and what it meant for her future.

To her shock, Melissa and Maddie hardly seemed surprised when she revealed her secret hookups with Ben. "We figured something was going on," Maddie said matter-of-factly.

"But how?" Shannon asked incredulously.

Melissa shrugged. "It's a small town," she said with a smile, going back to arranging some flowers in a vase.

"What should I do?" Shannon asked, desperate for advice.

"What do you want to do?" Maddie asked her, looking over at her friend as she arranged vintage books on a shelf.

"I want to try things out with him," Shannon said confidently. "I am just terrified to hurt Amelia, for him to realize that I am not really meant to be a mom and that he will ditch me."

Maddie and Melissa stopped what they were doing to stare at Shannon with skeptical looks on their faces.

"Why would he ever think that?" Melissa asked her. "You love Amelia more than you've ever liked any kid. You two get along great."

"Well, yeah," Shannon said, "But I'm not exactly a mother figure."

Melissa pondered this, taking a minute to think through her response. "I wasn't sure that I would ever be a mom. With our past," she said, nodding at Maddie, "I wasn't sure if that was a good idea, if I would have what it takes to be a good parent. When I met Jakob, I knew that I wanted to have his babies. He's such a good man, so perfect for me. When I got pregnant, I never looked back. I don't have a doubt in my mind that my past has nothing to do with my future. If anything, it will make me a better parent. I have seen firsthand what not to do."

Shannon came over and rubbed Melissa on the back as she wiped away tears from her face. Shannon knew that this was a lot for Melissa to do and she had a lot of changes in her life. She admired Melissa for being so brave and so confident, for knowing at the end of the day that everything was going to be okay.

"There's no one right or wrong way to be a mom. As long as you love that child more than anything in the world, more than your own life, you will be okay," Melissa said, her maternal side already shining bright.

Shannon nodded. It was a lot to think about, a great deal to ponder. She truly did not know what the future held for her, but she knew that she needed to have more confidence in herself. She portrayed a very confident person on the outside, from her wild outfits to her sassy piercings and haircut, but she needed to remind herself that she needed to have that confidence throughout her entire being. And with that, the girls called it a night, embracing each other before parting their ways and going home to their own lives.

Returning His Power

Chapter 15

Shannon was having a quiet Friday morning going through applications for the position of breakfast chef when Barb came rushing into the coffee shop, looking frantic as ever.

"Shannon!" She said, a sigh of relief in her voice. "Thank goodness I caught you."

Shannon stood up from the stool behind the counter. "What's up, Barb?" Shannon asked, immediately concerned that something was wrong with Amelia.

"I am in quite the pickle," Barb said, walking up to the counter.

"Oh?" Shannon asked. "Can I help?"

"That's exactly what I came here for," Barb explaining, pushing her salt and pepper hair out of her face. "I promised my sister that I would come and stay with her tonight while her husband recovers from a hip replacement, but I had no idea that Ben is already obligated to work overnight. I can't leave Amelia home alone, and there's no room for her in my sister's tiny senior apartment. Would you...could you..." she began.

"Barb, it would be my pleasure to stay with Amelia if you'd like," Shannon said, more than willing to spend time with her little bestie.

Barb jumped and down and clapped her hands together. She came around the counter to sweep Shannon up in a big hug, swaying back and forth. "Oh thank you, sweetie," she said. "I owe you big time."

"It's no trouble at all, really," Shannon said. "Now let me get you a coffee and let's catch up." The woman smiled and accepted a mug from Shannon, sitting down at the counter to begin describing her sister's crotchety husband.

As she pulled into Ben's driveway, she saw his truck parked by the garage. She grabbed her overnight bag filled with movies and her pajamas and another bag from the coffee shop with chocolate chip cookies for Amelia. As she walked up the path, she expected Amelia to swing open the front door and greet her, but she did not show up.

She waited patiently after pressing the doorbell. When a minute went by, Shannon was about to press it again when the door opened a crack. Ben saw her, pulled his head back in surprise, then opened the door wider.

"Shannon," he said, a smile on his face. "What are you doing here?" As he pulled the door open further, she saw that his hair was pushed back, his forehead glistening with sweat. Her gaze trailed down, biting her lip as she realized that he was shirtless and in nothing but a pair of gray sweatpants which left very little to the imagination.

Her eyes focused in on his tight, rippled abs, then lowered more, her heart clenching as she became intimately familiar with the outline of his cock.

"Shannon?" Ben asked again. Shaking her head, she managed to tear her gaze from his manhood and looked back up at his face. He was smiling at her mischievously, knowing that he caught her staring.

"Oh, oh!" Shannon said. "I'm here to babysit. Don't you need to get to work?" She asked, confused as to why he wasn't ready to head out.

"Babysit?" Ben asked. "What are you talking about?"

"Barb came into the shop today and told me about her sister's husband and that you need to work tonight, so I agreed to watch Amelia." She explained.

Ben groaned and shook his head. "Mom was all excited about wanting to take Amelia to the Dells this weekend to go to a waterpark. Her sister's husband is fine," he said. "I think we've been set up."

Shannon had to laugh at Barb's creativity. "So Amelia and Barb are gone?" she asked.

Ben nodded. "They left right after school today and are coming back on Sunday morning." Opening the door wider, Ben moved to the side so that Shannon could come in. "It's cold out there, come on in while I get changed," he said.

Shannon followed Ben inside, unable to stop herself from staring at his ripped, muscled back. A trail of sweat dripped down his spine, catching in the small of his back. His pert, muscled ass looked absolutely smackable in the sweatpants and Shannon resisted the urge to reach out and grab it.

Ben walked into the kitchen and poured himself a glass of water and one for Shannon while he was at it. He stood in front of the sink, gulping it down as Shannon watched his Adam's apple bob up and down. She never thought about it before, but watching Ben drink water like it was going out of style was definitely her new kink.

"I'm sorry about my mom," Ben said as he set the empty glass on the counter. "She shouldn't have done that," he said regretfully.

Shannon smiled. "Don't apologize. I think it's really cute," she said. "And lucky for you, I now have plenty of chocolate chip cookies to go around," wagging the bag in front of him.

Ben snatched the bag from her, a huge smile on his face. He dug into the bag and bit into a cookie, moaning as he slowly chewed it. "Why are you so perfect?" he said quietly, taking another bite.

Shannon laughed. "I hardly think that I am perfect, but I think I will let you get away with thinking so." She slipped off her jacket and set it on the back of a chair, then took a seat at one of the stools in the kitchen.

Ben looked over at her from across he counter, then winked at her cutely when there was nothing left to say. Shannon smiled as she stare over at him.

"Sorry I interrupted your workout," she said to him.

"Darlin'," Ben began, "I can think of a million better ways to workout than to lift weights in my basement, and they all involve you naked in my bed," he said.

She hated to admit that she so easily turned to putty around him, but she was completely and totally hooked on Benjamin Kennedy.

"I'm going to go shower," Ben said, "I'm pretty gross right now. Want to stick around and I'll make you dinner?" He asked.

"I definitely do," Shannon said, "But I have an important question that's going to impact my decision."

"Ask me," Ben said, leaning down on the counter.

"Did Barb teach you how to cook?" She asked, a smile forming on her face.

Ben burst out in a laugh, pulling the tie out of his hair and shaking it loose. "I can promise you that Barb taught me how to boil water. Everything else I learned from TV and books," he said as he strode upstairs.

"Thank goodness," Shannon said. "Then I'll stay."

"I knew you would," Ben called out from upstairs. "See you in a bit." She heard the bathroom door close and the shower start up, trying her absolute best not to picture Ben naked.

She, of course, failed at that task and as she sat at the kitchen counter, swirling the water around her cup, she imagined Ben upstairs, the hot water pelting down on him, rubbing soap up and down his body, his hands gliding slippery along his muscular angles and curves.

She imagined him with one hand against the

shower wall, the other firmly on his cock, getting himself off thinking about fucking her as he tugged his hard manhood, his calloused hands jacking it up and down.

Shannon snapped out of her fantasy as she heard the water shut off upstairs and the shower door open and close. She stood up, grabbed a chocolate chip cookie and took a huge bite, trying to shut up her filthy imagination with sugar.

Ben came down a few minutes later, now in a pair of jeans and a long sleeve black cotton shirt. His hair was freshly styled and she had to smile at her cute, metrosexual guy. She reached up and cupped his cheek, then stood on her tiptoes to give him a quick peck on the cheek.

"What was that for?" Ben asked as she stepped down and walked into the living room.

"For being so damn cute," Shannon said with a laugh, collapsing onto the couch.

Ben came and laid next to her on the couch, stretching out his tall body next to hers. Shannon remembered their first night together on the loveseat in her office, which seemed like just yesterday even though so much had happened since then.

Ben nestled in closer to her, his head leaning against hers as their bodies merged together. They were like this for a few minutes in silence, before Shannon began gently nudging Ben.

"What do you want me to do?" Ben said with a laugh as she accidentally elbowed him in the ribs.

"Turn around," Shannon said.

"So you'll be spooning me?" Ben asked.

"Yeah," Shannon said, hugging the couch as Ben flipped his big body around so that he was facing away from her.

"I've never been the little spoon before," he said hesitantly.

Shannon wrapped her arms around Ben, kicking her leg over his and hugging him tight. They probably looked ridiculous as her small body tried to envelop his, but she attempted it anyway. "Everybody needs to be the little spoon every once in a while," Shannon said matter-of-factly.

They laid in silence for some time, Ben clutching Shannon's hands against his chest, listening to each other breathing. Suddenly, Shannon was overcome with need, wanting nothing more than to be even closer to Ben. She climbed on top of him, balancing on his hip before he flipped to his back.

She straddled his waist, feeling his cock poking at her ass as she leaned down to kiss Ben. "Let's go upstairs," Shannon whispered to him, almost a question.

Ben nodded and stood up, helping Shannon get to her feet before leading her up the stairs. When they reached his room, he closed the door behind them, then stripped his shirt off. Shannon pulled off her sweatshirt and tugged off her leggings, leaving her in a simple black bra and pair of purple panties. Ben looked down at her, taking in her body, and growled.

He walked towards her, wanting to take everything that Shannon was offering. Shannon pulled his body against hers by his hips, reaching back to grab his tight ass as she popped up to kiss him. She smacked his ass and Ben smiled, his cock pushing into her stomach.

She pushed Ben on the bed, which was no small feat given their size difference. She crawled up his naked body, feeling the heat that he gave off. She wanted to show him how much he meant to her, how much she appreciated his patience and thoughtfulness.

"Wait—" Ben said, holding up a hand to her. Shannon immediately stopped and listened to hear what he had to say. "Are you sure you're ready, after your surgery?"

Shannon smiled and pondered the thought. "I feel fine," she said, "but I promise to say something if it doesn't feel right." Ben seemed satisfied with her answer and laid back down, letting her climb on top of him.

Dragging her fingernails up and down his chest, Shannon moved slowly down his body, taking his cock in her mouth. He groaned as she lubed his cock up with her tongue, using her spit to slide her lips quickly up and down his shaft.

Ben moaned as he thrust his hips forward, leaning into Shannon's delicious mouth. The groans coming from his lips escalated as Shannon took him deeper, further than she'd gone before.

Shannon kissed his hips, grasping Ben's cock and stroking him, placing pressure on all the right places. Ben growled through gritted teeth as he grabbed her underneath her arms and hiked her up to him, so that they were face-to-face. He flipped her onto her back, then leaned over to the nightstand to grab a condom.

Sliding the condom on, he grabbed her hips and lined himself up above her. Slowly, gently, he dipped his head down, plastering kisses on her forehead, her cheeks, her neck. He nibbled on her earlobe, then licked her neck before giving it a quick bite.

Shannon loved the way his lips moved over her body, never staying in one spot long. The way his hands managed to glide up and down her, grasping her hips, her breasts, her ass, she could hardly get enough of his touch.

Ben reached down and brushed Shannon's pussy, finding her blissfully wet and ready for him. Gently, he pressed his cock into Shannon, wanting to savor every second. His pleasurable moans as he dove into her escaped his mouth into the room, and Shannon matched it with gasps of passion as well.

Slowly, he began to thrust into her, continuing to kiss her neck over and over again. Shannon reached up to grasp Ben's face to kiss him, nipping at his lips between her gasps and sighs.

As their bodies fit together like missing puzzle pieces, they leisurely worked up to the point of no return, riding the wave of a simultaneous orgasm, allowing themselves to make as much noise as they wanted in the empty house.

Sated, and completely exhausted from the pleasure, Ben eventually lifted himself off of Shannon, hoping that he wasn't crushing her beneath his weight. She appeared positively smitten, and whined a bit as he pulled away from her. He quickly pulled her into his arms, wrapping her up in a way that she never felt more protected, more safe.

Shannon was overcome with emotion after the orgasm, and never wanted Ben to let go of her. Lucky for her, they stayed that way the entire night. When she woke up the next morning, Ben's arms were still around her, a smile on his face.

The bathroom was full of steam after Shannon's exorbitantly long shower at Ben's house the next morning when she heard her phone ringing from the bedroom. Opening the door and wrapping the towel tight around her body, her eyes grew wide as she realized her mother was FaceTiming her.

Answering the video call, Shannon tried to hide the background behind her as much as she could. "Hey honey!" Her mom said, "Where are you?" She asked, immediately knowing that Shannon wasn't at home.

"I'm uh..." Shannon began, at a loss for a lie to make up.

Before she could stop him, Ben walked into the bedroom in just a pair of briefs with a plate of bacon and eggs for her. "Oh dear lord!" Celeste said with shock, and a bit of glee. Celeste had a saucy grin on her face as she looked at Shannon. "Well, well, well," she began. "I don't suppose you want to invite the new police chief to our lunch today, do you?"

Shannon groaned as she turned her camera off, Ben laughing in the doorway. "I will ask him, Mom, okay? Talk to you soon," she said, ending the call as quickly as possible.

"I am so sorry!" Shannon shouted, throwing the phone on the bed.

Ben was holding onto the doorknob laughing way too hard for just being caught by Shannon's mom in nothing but a pair of underwear.

"Your mom is maybe as bad as mine," he said.

Shannon was relieved that Ben wasn't upset, and lightened up a bit as she watched him laugh. "Do you want to come along?" Shannon asked.

Ben nodded. "I just have to run into the station this morning but after that, there is no place else I'd rather be."

Shannon appeared positively pleased as she sat on the bed in her towel, smiling and Ben delivered her breakfast in bed.

"I have one important question, though," he said seriously.

"Oh?" Shannon asked, worried about what he was going to ask.

"Does your Mom like roses or tulips?" he asked her, a smile on his face.

This was it, Shannon deduced. She had officially caught feelings for Ben.

Returning His Power

Chapter 16

Shannon nervously prepared for family brunch, going through her closet for the perfect outfit. She settled on a tan pencil skirt and an emerald blouse with a pair of blue flats. Ben was going to pick her up after he was done at work, and she nervously fiddled with the buttons on her blouse as she waited to hear his truck pull into her driveway.

She was nervous for Ben to meet her family. She had not had a man over to her parents' house since her ex-husband, and that seemed to be ages ago. She recalled how her mother pulled Shannon aside, voicing her concerns to her about Shannon's ex, begging her to reconsider the wedding. Shannon, at the time, was young and even more headstrong, pushing off her mother's concerns.

Shannon remembered the hurt on her father's

face when she told him that she was divorcing Peter, knowing that she let him down. She never wanted to see him like that again. More than anything, Shannon was terrified that they were going to see some major red flag with Ben that she was not noticing.

A few minutes later, Ben pulled up, leaving his truck running as he ran up to the front door to collect Shannon. He walked her over to his truck, opening the passenger door for her and helping her up into the lifted truck.

As they drove out to Shannon's parents' house in the country, Ben reached down and clutched her nervous hand in his, squeezing it tightly. She could not help but smile at his sweet gesture, leaning over to kiss him on his freshly-shaven cheek.

Ben was dressed smartly in a pair of dark gray dress pants and a tailored checkered dress shirt. He wore a nice pair of dress shoes. Shannon appreciated his fashion sense and attention-to-detail, happy to have found someone who enjoyed clothes nearly as much as her.

As they drove up the winding driveway, Shannon seemed to be much more nervous than Ben, who casually parked the truck, then reached in the backseat for the roses for Celeste.

Shannon stepped out of the truck and eyed up all of her brothers' pick-ups. She mused that Ben's big black beast of a vehicle looked quite at home in the fleet of trucks.

When they stepped inside the back door, they came face-to-face with a kitchen crowded with Romanos, all staring at the door eagerly awaiting

Shannon and her date.

Her brothers clutched cans of beer and eyed Ben suspiciously, their wives nodding at Ben appreciatively. Three screaming kids came running into the kitchen, breaking up the deafening silence. With that, everyone began talking, walking up to Shannon and Ben and reintroducing themselves after meeting in the hospital.

Celeste gave Ben a big hug when he presented her with the roses, and even Phil Junior seemed to look impressed at the gesture, which was quite difficult to pull off.

Everyone talked over each other, but Ben fell effortlessly into the conversation, bending down and talking to each of the nine children, pulling his badge from his pocket and letting them all touch it.

When she looked up, Celeste was at the stove buttering garlic bread, a sweet look on her face as she patted her heart.

As they sat down for lunch, Ben answered all of her brothers' questions, making eye contact with her father often.

Everything was going shockingly well, so when they were clearing the table after lunch and her father asked to speak to Ben outside, Shannon nearly crawled into a ball and died.

Ben followed her father outside. She watched them out of the big living room window, and they appeared to just be talking about her father's landscaping and patio, pointing at various features underneath the melting snow.

Her breath began to steam up the window in front of her and Shannon tore her gaze from the two, going back into the kitchen to dry dishes and keep herself busy. She caught her mother sneaking whiffs of the roses as she put leftovers in containers, humming to herself.

"What do you think?" Shannon asked her mother and her three sisters-in-law. They all looked at each other in silence, then nodded to each other. "What?" Shannon asked frantically. "Bad?" She asked, worried.

"He's so great, honey," Celeste said sweetly. "Just the way he can handle your brothers and the love that he has for his daughter. You can tell that you really have somebody special on your hands."

Shannon smiled at her mother's positive review of Ben, shocked and relieved that things seemed to be going so well. Her sisters-in-law all agreed with her, citing how he saved her life. "Plus he's not bad to look at either," Celeste said, smiling devilishly. "But you already know that," she said with a wink.

"Mother!" Shannon chastised, throwing a towel at her mother playfully. The women all erupted in laughter, drowning out the noise of kids destroying the tidy living room.

After lunch dwindled down, Shannon and Ben said their goodbyes. Once they were on the road, Shannon could not hold back any longer. "What did you and my dad talk about?" she asked him.

"That's personal!" Ben said jovially, running his hand through his hair.

"What do you mean, personal?" She asked. "It's my dad!"

"We were just having a guy conversation," he said casually. "You know, dad to dad," he explained.

Shannon sighed, exasperated with trying to get details from him, eventually just giving up. When they got back to her house, Ben was able to appease Shannon with kisses, both on her mouth and other delectable places.

Monday morning came way too quickly for Shannon's liking, but she was excited to have the chance to catch up with Maddie on her break. Maddie sipped on her peppermint mocha as she walked through the new kitchen with Shannon. "It's amazing," Maddie said, watching Shannon put away various pots and pans. They discussed the lack of applications for the chef job, and Maddie promised to hang up more help wanted posters at the library.

"Speaking of the library," Maddie said. "I've seen your man in the library quite a bit lately," she said matter-of-factly.

"Oh?" Shannon said, curious about what Ben was doing at the library. It was usually Barb who took Amelia to storytimes, but she supposed he took her every once in a while.

"Yeah, usually in the early afternoon he comes in, takes a few things out," Maddie said off the cuff.

"What kinds of things?" Shannon asked, inching up to her friend curiously.

"Now, Shannon, you know that I am not allowed to disclose a patron's personal check-out history," Maddie said sternly, wagging her finger at Shannon.

Shannon sighed heavily at this, wishing her friend would break the rules just this once to give her some intel.

"You know which author has been flying off the shelves lately?" Maddie asked innocently.

"Who?" Shannon said absentmindedly focused on putting cookie sheets in her new cupboards.

"Betty Friedan," Maddie replied, running her fingers along the new countertops.

"*The Feminine Mystique?*" Shannon replied. "Why would that be popular now?" she asked absentmindedly, focusing on the task at hand. Finally, realization hit her. "You mean to tell me that Ben checked out the most important publication in feminist history?" Shannon screeched, voice full of shock and awe.

Maddie hissed at Shannon, shushing her. "Will you keep it down?" She implored. "I said nothing! I was merely making a general observation."

Shannon stood up and leaned up against the counter, floored that Mr. Ben "I'm an alpha" Kennedy was reading a feminist manifesto.

"He must really like you," Maddie said seriously.

"Something like that," she said, shaking her head then reaching for a box of cooling racks to store away.

Later that day, Shannon was leaving work when she saw Ben parked down the street in front of The Hound Dog. He had his speed scanner out, looking to catch speeders on the main drag. She walked up to his window and he slammed the book he was reading shut, tossing it to the passenger seat, but not before she caught a glimpse of the title.

"Hmm," Shannon said as Ben rolled his window down. "*Raising Strong, Independent, and Well-Adjusted Girls in Today's Society*. Interesting reading material," she said slyly.

"Yeah, well, I need all the help I can get. The other day I asked Amelia to make her bed. She refused, telling me that she was under 'no obligation' to listen to men. Who do you think she got that from?"

Shannon gritted her teeth at this news, realizing that she probably should have clarified that, in this instance, Amelia should not think of her dad as a man. She made a mental note to explain it better to Amelia when they saw each other next.

"Sorry about that," Shannon said. "But surely you can appreciate the sentiment."

Ben nodded sarcastically at Shannon, but could not resist breaking into a smile. He leaned out the window to kiss her, not even caring that he got her pink lipstick all over his mouth.

"Officer Kennedy!" Shannon whispered. "Public displays of affection, really?" She chastised him mockingly.

Ben could do nothing but grin at Shannon, absolutely captivated by his woman. "It's Chief," he corrected, before furthering the conversation. "Can I stop by after work tonight?" Ben asked. "It will be late, probably around ten."

"Ooh," Shannon said. "You're always welcome, but you should know that I am already in bed at that hour."

"You usually don't go to sleep until midnight," Ben said quizzically.

"Yeah," Shannon said. "Who said anything about sleeping?" With a wink, she walked down the sidewalk to the post office, shaking her ass seductively, knowing that he was watching her every move.

Ten o'clock could not arrive fast enough for Shannon. She paced through her bedroom, listening to the clock tick tock slowly.

After changing her nightgown three times, she settled on a spaghetti strap number with leopard print. The quiet knock on her front door alerted Shannon as she was sitting in her living room, pretending to be reading a magazine. She walked to the front door, opening it and finding Ben's smiling face.

He stepped inside, running his eyes up and down her body. "You look beautiful," he said to her.

"And you look quite handsome yourself," she said, pushing up on her toes to reach his lips. Ben barely had the front door closed before she was dragging him upstairs to her bedroom, needing to feel his touch on her bare skin.

She giggled as she pulled him into her bedroom, which was sexily illuminated with candles. She sat back on the bed as she watched Ben slowly strip off his uniform.

He pulled his holster off and set it gently on one of her tables. Then, facing her with a saucy grin, Ben began to slowly unbutton his shirt, making her drip with anticipation.

As Ben reached the last button, he pulled the shirt out of his pants and stripped it off, standing in a white tank top and his uniform pants. Shannon had to check to ensure that her tongue was not hanging from her mouth as he continued the striptease, slowly pulling the tank top off.

Shannon stuck her hand out, waving her finger in a come hither motion. Ben walked over to her, waiting for Shannon to make the next move. She leaned over the edge of the bed, grabbing onto his belt loops, tugging him towards her. The top button of his pants was already undone. Carefully, she caught his zipper pull between her teeth and slowly dragged it down.

She could feel his erection on her forehead as Shannon kept her teeth together, pulling the zipper all the way down. With a groan, Ben naturally thrust into her face. Shannon pulled his pants down, inhaling his manly scent. She snapped her fingers, sitting up and motioning for him to continue stripping.

Ben grabbed his package, cupping it in his hands and stroking it through his briefs. Shannon sat back and watched his every movement, pleasure running through her veins.

Tucking his thumbs in the band, Ben bit down on his bottom lip as he made eye contact with Shannon, not breaking the stare as he dove closer to her, stripping off his tight briefs, his cock popping out freely. He wrapped his hands around her head, gently grabbing her hair as he thrust his cock against her body. Climbing up on top of her, he began thrusting against her stomach, then her breasts as she laid down and watched him writhing on top of her.

He slid down her body, kissing and licking her belly and hipbones as he slid her silky nightie up. When he reached her panties, Ben pressed his mouth against her pubic bone, breathing hot air through her panties. When he broke contact, he stripped the panties off of her, nearly ripping them off of her body.

Ben licked her sensitive skin, then blew on it, the cold on her skin sending a spark up Shannon's spine. She was certain that there was nothing more incredible than this feeling. Ben easily grabbed Shannon's legs and spread them widely apart, his face diving back between her legs, eager to taste her once more.

He licked and nipped at her pussy, his mouth diving as deep as he could. Shannon groaned as he ate her out, loving the feel of his mouth on her most sensitive spot. She had never felt this way with any other man. Then again, no other man had ever been so enthusiastic to bring her pleasure.

Ben held Shannon's legs open as he continued to feast on her, his tongue swiftly moving between her clit and her pussy, desperate to pleasure both. "Do you have any toys?" he asked eagerly before nipping at her clit.

"Bottom drawer," Shannon said breathlessly. She nearly whimpered as he sat up, the lack of his mouth leaving her feeling exposed. She stared at the ceiling as Ben rifled through her drawer, looking for just the perfect thing.

When he climbed back on the bed, Shannon drew in a quick breath as she first heard—then felt—the strumming of her trusty vibrator. Ben turned it up to the fastest setting on her clit, his mouth settling in on her pussy, his tongue dedicated to lapping up her sweet juices.

Shannon was unable to resist thrusting up towards his mouth and the vibrator, following the sources of pleasure. As an orgasm built up inside of her, Shannon reached around her for anything to hold onto, grasping on her quilt to brace herself for the energy that would surge through her body.

As the orgasm swept through her, she clenched her legs around Ben's head, pressing tightly around him as he continued to lick her and angle the vibrator on her clit. When she couldn't take it anymore, he pulled the vibrator off and tossed it onto the bed, leaning forward to envelop Shannon in a passionate kiss.

When Shannon recovered, she grabbed the vibrator from the bed and turned it on, dragging it first around Ben's nipple then moving it lower, against his belly and his abs. When she began to run it over his hip bones, he began to shake, his breath growing unsteady.

Shannon smiled devilishly as she ran the vibrator over his erect cock, swirling it around the base, then teasing it along the shaft. Ben could not stop himself from reaching out and grabbing Shannon's hands, wanting to control the vibrator himself.

Shannon stood up and shook her head. She reached down and grabbed something out of her drawer, pulling out a pair of pink fuzzy handcuffs and hanging them on one finger. Ben looked at what she had and laughed breathlessly. Shannon climbed on top of him, grabbing his wrists and quickly securing them in the handcuffs above his head.

When she began gliding the vibrator over his cock once more, she smiled as he writhed underneath her, desperate for relief from the sweet torture. Before she realized it, his hands were free once more, having torn the handcuffs in half with just his strength.

With a *tsk*, Shannon stood up. She would need something more... professional for Ben. She reached for the handcuffs from Ben's holster, then winked at him as he threw his head back, tearing the old handcuffs off his wrists.

When she climbed atop him again, Ben gave into the sweet submission, wanting this more than anything. When she secured the cuffs to his wrists, Shannon grinned as she bounced on top of his cock, rubbing her pussy against it.

She slid a condom on his cock before stripping off her nightgown, tossing it to the floor. Ben whimpered as she got up on her knees, her pussy breaking contact with his shaft. He had relief when she sat back down, sinking down on his cock in one fast motion.

Shannon rode Ben's cock hard, more fervently than ever before. She wanted to tease him, to show him what she was capable of. When she ground down on his cock while also bouncing up and down on his shaft, reaching down to gently cup his balls, Ben could hardly see straight, his moans of pleasure filling the room.

There was nothing that could break their connection. Ben knew his place, that he was submitting his pleasure to Shannon, this fucking entirely in her control. He loved to watch her take charge, calling the shots for what was going to happen next.

"You like this pussy?" Shannon asked him in-between grinding on his dick.

"Yes," he moaned through his teeth.

"Yes *what*?" She asked, reaching down to clutch his pec and squeeze it as she ground down harder on his cock.

When he didn't answer, Shannon began to sit up higher on her knees, her pussy moving further and further away from Ben's cock.

"Yes, ma'am," Ben shouted out. "I love your pussy," he exclaimed. Satisfied, Shannon sank down on his cock and moaned a sigh of pleasure at the feeling.

Ben continued to groan and writhe underneath her, his wrists fighting each other as they were clasped together above his head.

When she felt him coming closer and closer, Shannon reached down and began to touch her clitoris, rubbing it quickly as she bounced up and down, bringing herself to orgasm as she fucked herself with his cock.

"Come for me," she said to Ben, ordering his pleasure.

"Yes, ma'am," Ben said, loving his place beneath Shannon. With four quick thrusts, Ben spilled inside of her, sweat on his brow glistening in the candlelight.

Shannon slid off of Ben's lap, quickly rifling through his pants pocket for the handcuff keys. Finding them, she crawled over to his outstretched arms, swiftly unlocking the cuffs. When he was free, Ben moved his arms down and gently massaged his wrists.

Shannon moved down and caught one of his wrists in her hands, reaching for some lotion from her bedside table and massaging it into one wrist, then the other.

"Did you like that?" She asked him, wanting to know Ben's true opinion about submission.

With a glow surrounding him, Ben looked over at Shannon. "Every single time we've been together is better than the last, and this was no exception. That was the hottest thing I have ever done in my life," he said earnestly, leaning forward to kiss her on the cheek.

Shannon had to sigh a breath of relief at hearing it, so glad to know that Ben enjoyed everything as much as she did. As they got under the covers, snuggling together, the two whispered to each other.

"You know you can always tell me anything, especially if there is something you really don't like, or maybe something you especially liked," Shannon said to Ben as they peered into each other's eyes, nose to nose.

"And the same goes for you," Ben said. "And that's not just in the bedroom, either. If I ever do anything to frustrate you, just let me know so we can talk about it and I will do my best to not do it again."

"So is now a good time to talk about your disgusting ability to eat everything and still look like this?" Shannon asked.

Ben smiled at her, then leaned into her playful slap on his bicep. They stayed like that for some time, until Ben got up early in the morning and put his clothes on, needing to get home before Amelia woke up. Before he left, he kissed Shannon on the forehead and tiptoed out of the room, hoping to not wake her up. When Shannon woke up alone the next morning, she could feel the absence of Ben in her bed, in her arms, and wished more than anything that she could wake up next to him each day.

Chapter 17

Shannon and Ben continued to sneak around like a couple of teenagers fooling around in their parents' houses until they both seemed to mutually realize that they literally had no reason to do so. Soon, Shannon began spending one night a week at Ben's house, earning the quiet approval of Barb as she enthusiastically waved to Shannon from her balcony when Shannon left in the mornings before Amelia woke up.

Once it began to warm up outside, Ben took Amelia to the park to push her on the swingset, then sat down with her on a bench and explained that Shannon would be sleeping over at their house sometimes. Amelia was tickled pink at the thought of getting to have breakfast with Shannon each day and requested movie sleepovers in the living room.

Shannon breathed a sigh of relief after hearing how well Amelia took the news, wanting more than anything to keep Amelia happy. She had already resigned to tell herself that if Amelia was uncomfortable with her sleeping over, she would just continue to see Ben in private, not taking the relationship any further.

Shannon's family caught on pretty quickly that things were escalating between she and Ben. They invited Ben, Amelia, and Barb over for their family lunch. Amelia was thrilled at the idea of making new friends, and quickly got along with Shannon's nieces and nephews, who she had not yet met.

Barb and Celeste became fast friends. Barb complimented Celeste's cooking so often that Celeste took Barb under her wing, showing her quick and easy Italian recipes. Barb and Celeste were an unstoppable force of motherly love.

It was more than a little adjustment to go from spending all of her time at the coffee shop to eagerly awaiting the first moment she could pull away from work to go to Ben's house to see him and Amelia. Her main focus at work was trying to find a good chef to roll out the new breakfast menu, but still had not found anyone.

Shannon was restocking baking supplies when Jodie walked into the kitchen, meekly walking up to her.

"Shannon?" Jodie asked quietly.

Shannon wiped her hands on apron, then turned to face the young girl. "Yeah Jodie, what's up?" Shannon asked, ready to answer any of her questions.

"I would like to talk to you about the job, the cooking job," Jodie said.

Shannon nodded, not even considering that Jodie would be interested in something so intense. "Let's go sit," Shannon said, leading Jodie to her office.

She sat down and listened to what Jodie had to say. "I know that I'm just sixteen, but I have already completed all of my studies and passed my GED," Jodie said. "I love working here, and I want to prove to you that I can do this," she said.

Shannon leaned forward, sympathetically looking at Jodie. "But Jodie," Shannon said. "would your mother be okay with this? Isn't it tough on her already that you are working here at all?"

Jodie nodded. "It is really hard for Mama to see me leave the house and work outside the home. But we had a good discussion, she and I. She said that she will support me in whatever decision that I make, that she wishes that things could have been different with Jakob when he wanted to leave."

Shannon nodded, familiar with Jakob's background and the tumultuous excommunication that Jakob faced from leaving the Amish community.

Shannon stood up, pushing her exercise ball chair back. Jodie stood up as well, rubbing her hands on her blue dress. Shannon held out her hand, "Congratulations Jodie King. You're officially Grounded's new Breakfast Chef."

Clutching Shannon's hand, Jodie's face flushed with excitement, never wanting anything more in life than this.

Shannon locked up the coffee shop as soon as she

could, then drove a mile or so to Ben's house. Ben was still at work and Barb was preparing a salad for dinner. Amelia was excited to see Shannon, telling her all about her day. When Ben came in, he walked up to Amelia and kissed her on the cheek, then kissed Shannon on the cheek. Barb stood against the counter, eating her salad and smiling contentedly as she watched her son.

When Ben was tucking Amelia in that night, Shannon heard her calling her name. She walked into the girl's room and sat down next to Ben on her bed.

"Shannon, I just needed to tell you something. I really like it when you're here. When you sleep at your house sometimes I wake up and miss you. I can just tell you're not here and I hate it," Amelia said quietly.

Shannon's mouth drooped down at the absolute adorableness of the little girl. "I feel the same way about you when I sleep at my house!" Shannon said truthfully. "It's so boring in the morning to eat my cereal alone without my bestie," Shannon said.

Amelia squirmed down under her covers more, beginning to get drowsy with sleep. "I wish that you could be here all the time," she said, before drifting off to sleep, her hair in two messy braids on her pillow.

Shannon and Ben stepped quietly out of her room, shutting the door behind her. When they were in Ben's bedroom, he walked up to her quietly.

"I feel the same way, you know," Ben said. "When you're not here or I'm working the night shift, it's just not the same without you."

The room seemed to close in around them, but in the best way possible. She felt cozy and comfortable as he stood in front of her, reaching out to grab her hands, stepping closer to her.

Shannon wrapped her arms around Ben, letting him hold her as they stood in silence for more than a few minutes, just allowing them to speak to each other without saying a word.

"You know I love you, right?" Ben whispered in her ear.

A single tear fell from Shannon's face as she tightened her embrace around Ben. "I love you so freaking much," Shannon said. "You're my everything," she admitted to him.

They stood together just like that for a little longer before climbing into bed together, falling asleep holding each other and waking up the exact same way.

Shannon reluctantly agreed to go to the mall with Maddie to help her shop for clothes for her upcoming trip to Scotland to see Nick. Although they had just seen each other in February, the distance was just too much for them and she managed to work enough extra hours to take a quick, four day trip to Scotland.

As they roamed through the mall, Maddie stopping to stare at outfits in every storefront's display, Shannon found herself walking over to a jewelry store display. She eyed the engagement rings and stared at them with wonder. She had never cared about rings before.

She happily gave Peter her wedding band and engagement ring back when they divorced, not caring a bit about the jewelry. Yet now, her heart did a little pitter-patter as she eyed up the rings, thinking about the possibilities for a future with Ben. Realizing that her own thoughts were enough to freak herself out,

Shannon quickly caught up to Maddie, eager to volunteer to hold piles of clothes for her to try on, anything to get her mind off of rings.

Chapter 18

Amelia's seventh birthday was quickly approaching and Shannon had never been more stressed out in her life. She naturally volunteered the coffee shop to be the location of her party. Amelia was excited to invite her classmates, many of whom she had won over with her kindness and charm in the past few weeks.

Shannon spent day and night working with Barb on details for the party, wanting everything to be absolutely perfect for the big day. While Shannon was usually a go with the flow kind of girl when it came to event planning, she was unhinged when it came to Amelia's party.

Barb's calm, grandmotherly demeanor managed to keep Shannon grounded as they led up to the big day.

The night before her party, Barb and Shannon were at the coffee shop getting it decorated.

As they hung pink and black streamers from the ceiling, Shannon and Barb got to talking about everything, from their histories to life in general.

"You know," Barb said, "Benjamin's father was everything I was looking for at the time. He was charming, witty, older and independent. I truly thought that he was everything I needed," she said, stepping onto a stool and taping some streamers up.

"As time went by, though, and when I got pregnant, he quickly showed himself to be the deadbeat he was," Barb said softly. "It was a hard lesson to learn that not everybody who comes into your life wants the best for you. He certainly did not, but without him, I wouldn't have gotten Ben."

Shannon nodded as she listened to Barb pouring her heart out. "I totally get what you mean," Shannon said. "So many people are not who they seem to be at first. I've made a lot of mistakes," she admitted, twirling an uninflated balloon in her hand.

"No matter what happens in life, no matter how bad it is, the only way to get through it is to move on eventually, or to at least have the courage to try," Barb said, stepping down from the ladder and placing her hand on Shannon's shoulder.

"I love you like a daughter, you know," Barb said. "The way that you've lit up my son's life—my granddaughter's life—has been the biggest and best gift that I've ever received. You're the mother that Amelia needs, that she deserves. I'm not always going to be around, but I know she will be able to count on you when I'm gone."

"Don't say that," Shannon said, tears streaming down her face. "You're going to be around forever."

Barb shook her head, wiping the tears from her face. "You don't realize how lovely you are, sweet sweet Shannon," she said, the wrinkles on her forehead sewn together as she held back more tears.

"If I ever have the honor—the privilege—of joining your family, it would be the most precious thing to ever happen to me," Shannon admitted to Barb.

Barb leaned over, pressing her forehead against Shannon's. "You will, sweetie. You will," she said. She pulled two tissues out of her pocket, handed one to Shannon and kept the other for herself.

The two women wiped their tears, then got back to business, moving tables around and setting up the piles of presents they had for Amelia.

Amelia's party was absolutely perfect. Children ran throughout the coffee shop, chasing each other with frosting all over their faces. The birthday girl was in seventh heaven, wearing not one but two feather boas and a brand new tutu that Shannon bought for her.

Ben stood proudly in a corner with the other parents, looking upon his little girl who was growing up in front of his eyes. He watched as she wore her tiara between her Princess Leia buns, running around chasing little boys. He was terrified of her growing up, but excited to see where she went in life.

Shannon poured cups of punch for the children, laughing as she cracked jokes to the kids. She wore a pair of black skinny jeans and a long sleeve pink shirt with matching pink flats. Her hair was beginning to grow out, just touching her shoulders. As she laughed, she arched her back, her eyes squeezed tightly shut as she let the laugh take over her body.

When Amelia opened her gifts, Shannon was sure to take oodles of pictures. Amelia loved the movie poster of *It Happened One Night* from Shannon, rushing up to hug her after she unwrapped it. Celeste and Phil came to the party, giving her a television and DVD player for her bedroom. Ben shook his head, smiling at the gift as Amelia's eyes flew open in shock. She was enthralled, and possibly Celeste and Phil's greatest fan.

When it began to rain, the parents moaned and groaned at the downpour. Instead of pouting, Amelia got a mischievous smile on her face, grabbing Shannon's hand and heading for the door.

Before allowing Amelia to pull her outside, Shannon grabbed an umbrella and insisted that Amelia use it, then followed her out. Amelia pulled Shannon on the sidewalk to a huge puddle. Jumping into the puddle, Amelia began screaming with laughter as she practically forced Shannon into the puddle. Relaxing for the first time that day, Shannon jumped in the puddle next to Amelia, clutching her hand as they screamed and kicked the water around.

After the party was over and the crowd broke up, Shannon put everything back, tearing down the decorations. It was, she realized, the perfect day. Amelia was so happy, which was all that Shannon wanted for her little buddy. She thought back to the early winter when they first met, hardly knowing anything about each other but having an instant connection.

Shannon thought back at how different she was then, how guarded and closed off she was to new people.

Now, though, she felt differently about things, perhaps more brave than ever before.

She knew there was a danger that went along to loving somebody too much, and realized that there was always a possibility that things with Ben could end up going south, but she honestly, in all of her pessimistic heart, could not imagine a day when that could happen.

Shannon truly loved Ben more than anything, laughing to herself as she thought back to her first impression of him. Sure, he remained to this day incredibly cocky and certainly overconfident, but there was so much more to him beneath the surface. She never knew there could be so much happiness in her life.

As Shannon locked up the coffee shop, she looked at how different it was. Her dream of having a full-service kitchen had finally come true. She spent her days managing an entirely new crew of waiters and waitresses and dishwashers. Jorge was bumped up to general manager, and Jodie was thriving in the kitchen, putting her entire heart into each plate of food.

Shannon realized, though, that while that dream of hers was spectacular—and she was so proud of herself for making it come true—there was so much more to life than the coffee shop and making a living.

As she drove to Ben's home, she eagerly made her way toward the people who made life so much more.

Returning His Power

Chapter 19

Shannon spent a beautiful, wonderful summer with the Kennedys. Amelia eagerly spent many days at the coffee shop, in charge of choosing movies to play on the projector. Shannon even took a few days off of work, spending days on the beach with Ben and Amelia as they built sand castles and swam in the calm Lake Michigan water. Barb took some time off to travel and have some solo adventures, which she enjoyed immensely.

Ben and Shannon had plenty of time to themselves as well. They managed to see each other even with their busy schedules. The new Village President hired another police officer so that Ben had more flexibility in his schedule. When he worked the night shift, though, he would tap on the window of the coffee shop late at night when Shannon was trying to catch up with all of her new payroll responsibilities and increase in orders with their booming breakfast launch. When Shannon heard the familiar tap on the window, she dropped her pen or slammed her laptop shut and went to greet Ben at the door, sweeping him into a big kiss.

The couple was disgustingly, blissfully happy. Sometimes they would even go out to The Hound Dog or The Billy Goat with the new officer and his wife, enjoying a night out on the town.

Their favorite nights, though, were those cuddled up at home, tucking in Amelia and spending hours talking about anything and everything. Shannon treasured these moments, never feeling more herself than when she was with Ben and Amelia.

She thought back to all the times in elementary and middle school when she would come home sobbing over kids teasing her because of her quirky clothes. She remembered spending hours trying to figure out different outfits so she would fit in, trying her best not to stick out like a sore thumb. No matter what she did, though, the kids still had something to say.

It was when she felt perfectly content that she thought of times like these, or when she and Ben were snuggling together late at night when a memory of her failed marriage flashed back into her mind.

It scared her that in her happiest moments that she thought of her worst memories, but Shannon realized that she was merely humbling herself. It was her soul reminding her that she had come so far, and that she deserved to be truly happy.

A week before Amelia was scheduled to go back

to school, Shannon took Amelia to the salon to get a haircut. Amelia was convinced that she wanted to chop off her braids and get short hair, but when the hairstylist went to cut it off, she started screaming, "No darling, no, don't do it!" so loudly that the stylist dropped her scissors, saving Amelia's treasured hair.

They returned home from the salon with a solid half inch cut from the bottom of Amelia's hair and a relieved child. Shannon would not trade these moments with her little buddy for anything. Even on days when she had a splitting headache or was overwhelmed with work, nothing made her happier than coming home to Ben and Amelia.

Ben organized a family photoshoot before the start of school with Melissa. Melissa, who was now fully showing and looking more gorgeous than ever, set up her camera on the beach at sunset. Ben, Amelia, and Barb stood on the beach, the beautiful sunset behind them. They all wore matching blue button down shirts. Jakob and Maddie came along to watch the photoshoot, curious to see Melissa in action.

It was a cool August evening, a slight breeze in the air. Shannon chased after Amelia with a hairbrush, trying to keep the wind from getting her hair in her face. Shannon was wearing a pair of white capris and a black tank top as she ran after Amelia on the sand, hairbrush and hairspray in hand. She was more than fine with her position behind the scenes, and wanted Amelia to be cooperative so that they could get this photoshoot over with.

Barb was laughing as Amelia ran around. Amelia stopped suddenly and turned around, smiling at something behind Shannon. Shannon caught up to

Amelia, then swirled around to see what she could possibly be looking at with such a grin.

On one knee in the sand was Ben, the love of her life, holding out a blue button down shirt. "Shannon Grant Romano," he said, tears in his blue eyes. "You are my everything. I didn't know how wonderful life could be without you in my life. Will you please join our family and marry me?" Shannon dropped the hairspray and brush onto the sand and slowly walked over to Ben. Amelia rushed up next to him, clutching his arm, a huge smile on her face.

"There is no question in my mind that I want to be your wife, to be with you always," Shannon said, reaching down to accept the shirt. She slipped her arms in the blouse, buttoning it up over her tank top. Barb stood behind Ben sobbing her eyes out. Maddie was crying as Melissa moved effortlessly around them snapping photographs. She could have sworn that Jakob was even crying a bit.

Ben stood up, then pulled a box out of his pants pocket. "I have this, too, not just the shirt," he said sheepishly as he brushed away tears from his face. Standing before her, he opened the delicate box to reveal a glorious ring with a rectangular cut blue sapphire ring surrounded by ten solitaire diamonds in a silver setting.

Shannon covered her mouth as she glimpsed the gorgeous ring. It was more perfect than anything she could ever dream up. Ben slipped the ring out of the box, then tenderly picked up her left hand, sliding it on her ring finger, a perfect fit.

Shannon threw her arms around Ben's neck, moving in for a kiss. Then she leaned down and pulled Amelia into their hug. Barb came over and joined the hug as well. Melissa urged them to look towards her for a photograph. As they smiled for a picture, Amelia tugged on Shannon's hand.

"Shannon?" Amelia asked Shannon, looking up to her expectantly.

"Yes, honey," Shannon said, peering down at her little buddy.

"Does this mean we get to be best friends forever?" The girl asked optimistically.

"Oh Amelia, honey," Shannon said, bending down to clutch the girl's face in her hands. "Forever and ever," she promised, pulling the girl into a warm embrace.

Returning His Power

Epilogue

Four months later

Crowds of people dressed in their winter finest walked into Willow Falls Public Library. Chairs were set up along the middle of the library between the stacks and stacks of books, with an aisle going through the center.

The circulation desk turned into a beverage center with hot toddies and hot chocolate on tap.

People eagerly mingled with each other, their voices filling up the typically quiet library. A loud cackle caught the ears of everyone in the room, leading their gazes to a curvy, redheaded middle-aged woman who was currently telling Barb what must be a hilarious story, her Scottish accent filling up the room.

Melissa stepped out of the quiet study room, closing the door softly behind her. The sleeping little girl in her arms, a beautiful three month old infant named Maggie Anne King, in honor of Melissa's late mother, Margaret, and Jakob's sweet mom, Anna. Melissa walked up to Jakob, who looked dapper in a tuxedo, and she handed the baby to him.

The baby looked even tinier in his arms. He leaned down to kiss her on her forehead, then reached out to kiss his wife as well before she picked up her camera and went to snap photographs. He was madly in love with each of them, the little girl in his arms and the woman who birthed her.

Ben Kennedy walked up next to Jakob, a smile on his face as he wore a matching tuxedo. They nodded at each other, and Ben smiled widely as Jakob offered the baby girl to him. Ben carefully took her in his arms, remembering the long nights when he would hold Amelia as she slept soundly.

Slipping out of the quiet study room, Shannon and Amelia walked hand-in-hand over to Ben. In a pretty winter dress and white shawl, Amelia peeked up at the baby and smiled. Shannon smiled at Ben and the baby, love in her heart, the blue ring shining on her finger next to another simple band. The two had married at the courthouse a month after their engagement, unable to wait before starting their life together.

The tight long sleeve red bridesmaid's dress that Shannon wore was unexpectedly tighter as she was showing a small baby bump. She pressed her hand on her belly, absolutely overjoyed at the miracle that her life had become.

They all sat down, taking their seats amongst

Barb, Shannon's parents, Jakob's family, and Nick's family from Scotland—even Gladys, of course—who fit in just perfectly with the American family and friends at the event. Jorge was cuddled with his new boyfriend, the local attorney, a tall redhead with a bushy beard who looked like he would be more comfortable cutting down a tree than standing around in a suit. Together though, they seemed to make the perfect pair.

Nick O'Shaughnessy began walking down the aisle as a violin commenced playing the wedding march. He looked dapper in his green plaid kilt and traditional black suit top.

The audience all stood up as they watched Maddie walk down the aisle. She looked beautiful in a princess wedding gown, with long sleeves and layers amongst layers of tulle poofing out below her waist. Her hair was swept up in a pretty bun, and she carried a bouquet of red roses and poinsettias.

As she walked down the aisle, finding it difficult to walk slowly when all she wanted to do was rush into Nick's arms, Nick pulled out a handkerchief and dabbed his eyes, unable to stop the tears from flowing as he saw his beautiful bride walk towards him. They fought so hard for their love and to be together, and they finally had the chance to make it happen.

They quickly recited a few vows of their own, a touching tribute to each other. Nick finished his vows by clutching Maddie's hands tightly, saying, "I was put on this earth to keep you warm at night, to make you smile when you are sad, and to do everything in my power to make you absolutely, completely happy for the rest of my days."

They sealed their vows with a kiss and the audience erupted in joy. All three girls—Melissa, Maddie, and Shannon—had found their real-life romance, their impossible dream men coming to life. As these men loved them, the women loved them back unconditionally. They may not have been the men they expected to end up with, but they were perfect in their own ways.

Melissa gladly handed off the camera to Ben as she came up alongside Maddie and Shannon. The girls clutched hands with each other, their respective rings sparkling off of the library's lights.

Ben held up the camera, "All right ladies," he said. "Say Wisconsin," he said.

"Wisconsin!" The girls all cheered, huddling together and smiling at the camera, the snapshot of them with their heads together and arms around each other effortlessly capturing their close sisterhood on the most perfect day surrounded by their loved ones. It turns out that sometimes, even if the universe tells you over and over again that it is impossible, everything really does work out in the end.

And they all lived happily ever after.

The End

About the Author

Jacqueline Francis is a small-town Librarian from Wisconsin. She has been fascinated with romance novels since she was a teenager. When not dreaming up swoon-worthy fictional men, she likes to read about them! Find out about what she is reading by following her on Instagram, @jackiereadsromance. *Returning His Power* is her third novel.